OATH OF GOD

a novel

OATH OF GOD

Luis) +
May God
continue to guide
your spiritual
path! Keep hand
working hand
May He bless you
in your future!
[signature]

YZABELLE JIMÉNEZ MARTÍNEZ

TATE PUBLISHING & *Enterprises*

Published by Tate Publishing & Enterprises, LLC
127 E. Trade Center Terrace | Mustang, Oklahoma 73064 USA
1.888.361.9473 | www.tatepublishing.com

Tate Publishing is committed to excellence in the publishing industry. The company reflects the philosophy established by the founders, based on Psalm 68:11,
"The Lord gave the word and great was the company of those who published it."

Book design copyright © 2011 by Tate Publishing, LLC. All rights reserved.
Cover design by Kellie Southerland
Interior design by Joel Uber

Published in the United States of America

ISBN: 978-1-61346-122-8
1. Fiction: Christian, General
2. Fiction: Biographica
11.06.28

DEDICATION

For my amazing, hard working, humble, supportive and courageous parents.

For my two brothers and sister who have each contributed a
piece of themselves to complete my intricate soul.

*Para mi Abuelito, que siempre supo que su nieta pondría Sayula
en el mapa.*

For the Holy Trinity

DEDICATION

For my amazing, hard working, humble, supportive and courageous parents.

For my two brothers and sister who have each contributed a
piece of themselves to complete my intricate soul.

*Para mi Abuelito, que siempre supo que su nieta pondría Sayula
en el mapa.*

For the Holy Trinity

ACKNOWLEDGEMENTS

Thank you, God, for Your promise, for guiding my faith to keep my promise to You, and for the courage to speak the truth!

Thank you, *Ma* and *Pa*, for all the support you have given to all your children, financially and spiritually. My acknowledgments could be a never-ending eddy of words, as your love and support for your children. The thickness of your souls is what holds our family together. Thank you, "Angel!" I miss you deeply, and receiving this book contract on your birthday was the best gift I could have ever shared with you! Thank you for always watching over me and visiting me in my dreams. Thank you, brother and sister, for teaching me to be open-minded, creative, and what the meaning of unconditional love is. I love you all very much! *Gracias Abuelito, por siempre creer en mi talento, por tu orgullo y apoyo. Te extraño mucho. Gracias Tio, por tu apoyo en mi talento.*

Thank you spiritual "A.A. friend" for lifting me with your God-given words to move on from any and all "enemy falls!" Without you building and rebuilding my hope, I know I would have given up on certain situations. Thank you, *comadre*, for your love, support, and friendship. Thank you, Maria, for always believing that I would be a great leader and for teaching me so much about our great Leader, Jesus! Thank you for inviting me inside your home, making me a part of your family prayer time, and for giving this little sister five little sisters of Christ!

Thank you to my soul mate for sharing your ambition with me and modeling how to visualize your dreams. Without that step I would have never made the decision for whom or what I would be writing; I would have never found Tate Publishing. I loved you then, today, and when we meet again.

Thank you, Tate Publishing, for taking such a generous chance with me. God had led me to you four years ago; since then I knew we would have a glorious partnership.

Thank you, Sisters of Sacred Heart Retreat Camp, for giving me the opportunity to learn and grow from your teachings, generosity, and patience. Thank you for giving me the opportunity to share my story. Here is where I learned that I can change one soul at a time and where God proved to me the value of my voice. Thank you everyone who has trusted and shared their courageous stories with me. Thank you to those that have shared their time, knowledge and wisdom with me, both in life and with the process of this book. Thank you, Andrew, for all your marketing support, patience and friendship.

Thank you, Paula White and Donald Miller, for writing your stories and influencing my spiritual growth. Thank you, Alanis Morissette, and Marshall Mathers, for showing me how to use writing as an emotional outlet and my voice to speak the truth.

TABLE OF CONTENTS

THE BEGINNING AND THE ACTS OF LUKE

In the beginning, when God created the heavens and the earth, the earth was a formless wasteland, and darkness covered the abyss, while a mighty wind swept over the waters...God created man in his image, in the divine image he created him; male and female he created them.

Genesis 1:1-2, 27

It came to me in a dream one day, a premonition, something that no matter how hard you try, you cannot change God's plan. He has a plan for all of us. Some of us who do not bother believing in Him will never win the battle of true happiness and eternity. Others of us hear, listen, and obey all of God's signs; our level of faith is almost phenomenal. We have no temptations or doubts as to what God wants from us and how He manages to provide peace and happiness within us so naturally. Then there are those of us in the middle. Those of us who believe and love God, who have faith throughout our journey of life as we get to know God through Jesus, but every once in a while we fall into our own selfish desires or the enemy's temptations, where we at times question, "Could this really be what God wants for me?" Or perhaps we ask, "Why isn't God listening to me?" I myself am guilty of the latter; how about you? What kind of believer are you? As much as we at times try to force what is not meant to be, or on the contrary, fight what is meant to be, God will always prevail; He knows best and He always has His reasons!

Nostalgically, I gazed out the window, teary eyed, leaving behind a miraculous experience truly planned by God to strengthen our relationship. My mind reminisced about the friends I had made, the experiences I had endured, and the chemistry created between me and Elijah, a young man who led me to recognize my own spiritual capacity. Despite my feelings for Elijah, the one experience that would live inside my heart forever of the place I was leaving behind was that it was where I truly met God.

As I slept, I felt something grab hold of me, or maybe it was someone; I found myself in a clouded nirvana. I felt an unfathomable force stroking my hair and heard the words *it is he* in my dream or in my thoughts. They clouded the visions of my mind and continued. *It is he whom you already know. You are to serve him in his life. You must love him, for he will always love you in return.* When I awoke, I wondered, was this dream in fact sent from God or just my imagination? It was Joan of Arc who believed that God's messages come to us through our imaginations. Most believers feel that if they have undeniable faith in something, God will prevail. That is when prayer is the most powerful. I would be lying if I said that I did not fall off my path from time to time, and I had even felt a few times that I was so spiritually and emotionally disconnected from God, because of my own selfish desires. However, I always knew that God had phenomenal plans in store for me and that it would be quite a challenging journey trying to accomplish them. I have always felt that He had expected so much from me, as He does all His children, even you.

God is always there, inside your heart and soul. So I knew that whenever I fell off of my path, God would find me, dust me off, and send me back on my way toward His kingdom. I knew this because He was never far. I may have fallen at times, but He was always able to lift me higher. I may have been weak, but He was always there to offer me His strength. I may have been afraid, but He has always given me courage and comfort. I may have suffered, but I never completely lost faith. And He never stopped loving me, nor I Him, just as God will never stop loving you, even when you feel you have let Him down. Even when you think you do not deserve His love. Even when you think He is not there or does not exist. God is there, in your heart and soul, waiting for you to seek Him.

I was skeptical of the visions that the Lord invoked in my dream. Although I felt that I had heard this message, the challenging part was obeying God. Despite the fact that I believed I would never find true love, that love was hard to give as well as receive, an emotion that existed due to fear, and that most men were unworthy of my trust, I began the life long journey of finding my plan from God through the word of the Lord. I believed in the message that the Lord sent me. Through the strength of faith to prove God's words, I endured all of His hardships.

My first recollection of my Catholic identity was my mother converting from a Presbyterian to a Catholic when she married my father. Of course, it is not a part of my memory from actual experience but a story told to me by both my mother and father, each from their own perspective. My father was a traditional Mexican Catholic, who had a priest for an uncle and a nun for a sister. And the tradition in his family was if you got a girl pregnant, then you must honorably marry her in a Catholic church. A marriage and three kids later, I was welcomed into the family; I was born Catholic. As a child, it did not mean much to me except the fact that I had visited almost every church in the state of Jalisco, a state in northern Mexico, where my father's pueblo was located and where we visited his family every summer. These were the best memories of my childhood. I do not recall a summer in which we did not drive from Chicago to Mexico. If you ask my brother or sister now what their best childhood memory is, they would say exactly what I would, "Going on the trip." So even though I was born and raised in America, I was a Mexican Catholic. I knew all my prayers in Spanish and had attended Spanish Mass throughout most of my life. I made all of my sacraments in Mexico, although I do not recall one catechism or confirmation class.

I was ten when I learned the peace that my mind, heart, body, and soul absorbed when sitting in a Catholic church. I remember being dressed in a pink crocheted outfit my aunt or grandmother made, and I felt like the perfect pretty little girl. My aunts had been surprised at my impeccable behavior; it must have been a first. As a child, most of my family members and teachers could probably tell you that I was hyperactive, impulsive and argumentative, but for some reason I could sit in a church for one straight hour and listen without being antsy, complaining, or talking. The church was my sanctuary. I was safe and secure; I did not need any defense mechanisms. I could sense something comforting there. I was typically disruptive and extremely sensitive, but church had a way of calming me, perhaps taming me.

Being raised in a southeast suburb of Chicago, Piano City, Illinois, to be specific, my Mexican Catholic identity came out once a week, every Sunday at St. Augustine's Church, where they had one Spanish Mass, and then eventually two, then three and so on, as the Latino immigrant population began to expand. We drove to Verde Altos, the city that contained the ever-growing Mexican community that was served by St. Augustine's Church. As a teenager growing up in a community and around people of other dominant cultures than my own, I saw my church as a lure to be around my peers of the same cultural background. I was involved in traditional Mexican folkloric ballet and the bilingual youth group. The church was a magnet that drew me into the search for my soul, not because of my Catholic identity, but because of my Mexican identity. And throughout time, our two-week summer trips to Sayula, Jalisco, my father's hometown in Mexico, would turn into two or three months of sanctuary time for me. My little corner of church would become an entire country. Mexico became my church, my sanctuary, where I could be a Mexican Catholic.

It took me a long time to understand what it meant to be Catholic, to learn that being Catholic was not my cultural identity, but the foundation of my entire identity and its existence. It took me a while to get to know God, and to understand that I exist because of His one hundred percent love for me. I had to learn to be at peace within myself, forgive people in my life, accept God's plan, serve His children, and be humble. I also had to learn that being a Catholic was the hardest thing to be. Throughout the story of my life, it is my Catholic identity that has saved and protected me from the enemy's temptations that could have led me to a life of condemnation.

I had just spent several months in Oaxaca, Mexico on a study abroad program through my university. I was getting journalistic experience by researching non-profit organizations that assisted in helping the city's poverty-infested children and improving my

Spanish skills. The Spanish credits would allow me to complete my BA from Saint Ambrose University, a small private Catholic university in Chicago. Chicago, where I had been raised, was now my plane's present destination. Although I had just ended a significant chapter in my life, I was ready for a new, life-changing journey.

When I first had the opportunity to study in Mexico, I was scared, yet eager and excited. My father, who was born and raised in Sayula, Jalisco, made it a priority to always keep his American children in touch with their Mexican culture and for them to know the importance of family and roots, regardless of the obstacles. Therefore, every year he and my mother would pack up their four children and drive to Texas, where my mother was raised, and then to my father's hometown in Mexico. Because of my father's efforts, I never saw these trips as vacations, but as a sanctuary. Mexico was a place where I could regain my peace and serenity, a place to get away from the fast-paced life in which I was raised. Although geographically, Oaxaca, the state that would change my soul, was further south of Jalisco, it was still closer to Sayula than Piano City.

I always set goals as to what I hope to achieve for each "chapter" of my life. The level of difficulty is unimportant. A goal is a way to guide myself and know that my plans coincide with God's expectations. The goals I particularly set for this journey would affect me physically, emotionally, and spiritually. As independent as I was, I knew that this trip would force me to become even more independent. From what I understood, I had to learn what it was like to be away from my family, because it was an important characteristic that God needed me to possess in order to complete a greater plan; I also saw this as an opportunity to see my relationship with Him grow. I was nervous about leaving home for so long, but I knew that I was serving God and He would watch over me like a good, loving Father would. Finally,

I saw this escape as a transition to leave behind unfinished business, and upon my return, it would no longer be lingering. It was an opportunity to let go emotionally of one specific man; his name was Luke.

I met Luke at a party about three years ago on a hot, late August night. My best friend, Judith, was having a party for her cousin Oscar. Oscar had just finished his four-year service in the Marines. She thought a party with mostly old high school friends would make him feel welcomed back into "regular society." I walked through the door of Judith's three-bedroom flat. I could tell it was going to be a fulfilling night when I felt as though I had walked into Boston's *Cheers*. I heard my name recited from all four corners of the room, people from high school that I had not seen in ages. I felt this hungry and heaving smile in my direction. He was a friend of my childhood neighbor that I had known since I was four. James introduced me to his friend.

"This is Leizel. She was my neighbor for a long time," said James.

He sucked up my hand like an eager vacuum, still with his hungry smile. "You were lucky to have had such a beautiful and sexy neighbor. My name's Luke," he said.

I was attracted to Luke's dark brown eyes, fair olive skin, strong chiseled jaw and high cheek bones at first sight. What intrigued me more about Luke was his spirited and charming smile that never allowed him to conceal his emotions no matter how hard he tried. It was something I admired about him, since I was good at concealing my feelings, especially when I was afraid of someone hurting them. Every time Luke looked or spoke to me, he had this, "Man, you are an amazing woman" spark in his eye and in his smile. He was lean and medium in height, a sturdy five-foot six, in comparison to my five-foot three figure. He had the kind of arms in which you always felt safe—strong, but not overbearing. He had a tender embrace and very soft and sensual hands. Our personalities were like magnets, instantly drawn to each other. We started out the encounter as the luckiest poker partners of the night. We ended the night looking into the stars together and sealing it with a kiss. The kiss was not just any kind of kiss either. It was the kind of kiss that you knew would lead to others just as tender and passionate. I had never kissed a guy on the same night I met him, but we had this connection that made us feel as though we had known each other all our lives—or as he put it, since "our born days." Kissing Luke was a spiritual charge; he ignited my soul. In between our interactions were long hours of conversation. I told him that I was presently at community college hoping to transfer to a four-year university and eventually get a degree in journalism. He let me in on him being a single father.

The next day, the world around us that I had not noticed the night before would tell me of my odd behavior. Judith, who was my best friend since we were twelve, could not believe my impulsive behavior with Luke. She had known Luke since grade school, which was longer than she had known me. She and I knew each other from church. We went to different grade schools but to the same high school. Judith was like my "A.A." sponsor, but when it came to falling spiritually. Anytime I felt lost on my path to follow God, it was Judith that would walk with me to help find my way back, and I would walk with her when she needed me. Although she was constantly struggling with being comfortable in her skin physically, she was a beautiful girl with a pale glowing complexion. Like Luke, she had a spirited, beautiful face. Her eyes and smile, more often than not, had an inviting glow that gave her the compassion to always want to help people. She was the kind of friend that encouraged my relationship with God, and I was able to do the same for her.

"What was up with you and Luke?" Judith asked. "I have never seen you act like that."

"I don't know," I said. "I know this sounds cheesy, but last night didn't seem real. Our kiss seemed …so…magical, passionate," I said.

"Wow!" she exclaimed.

"I know!"

"Well are you guys gonna talk again?" Judith asked.

"I hope so," I said.

"You hope so? Well, did you give him your number?"

"Yeah, I did," I said.

"Well, I guess we'll see what happens, right?" Judith said.

"Yeah, we'll see."

"I think he'll call you," she replied with optimism.

I felt Judith was holding something back, like she wanted to say more, only she knew me too well to know that what she or anyone else said never mattered. I did not like to hear people tell me anything that seemed hindering or negative. It was not in her nature to say anything negative anyway. Being friends with her made every situation feel as though there would always be a happy ending; she was faithful to God, to her family, and to her friends.

The next few days I waited for Luke's call. The night we met was so passionate and ideal that if we never spoke again, the one memory we shared was enough to keep me fulfilled for many days to come, maybe even a lifetime. But he had not failed me. He called three days later. That encounter turned out to be a six-hour phone conversation.

He spoke to me about his past. True, we were both young, but he had already lived through quite a lot. Although Luke and I went to the same high school, we had never encountered each other. For one, he was younger than I was. Secondly, school was not a priority for him and so his attendance was modest, and although it did not appear to be a priority for me, I knew I wanted a high school diploma and that I had to go on to college. Finally, he was involved with another girl. He was so involved with her that he became a teenage father at the age of sixteen. The most significant comment he made that night was, "I broke her heart first, and then she broke mine." I figured if he was the last one to be heart broken, chances were he still was. Because of his past relationship, he wanted to know about mine.

My first love was pretty damaging emotionally, but at least I did not have a reminder of it. I was sixteen the first time I fell in love and was locked emotionally in this relationship for four years. He was a year ahead of me in school. I surrendered myself to him, physically and emotionally. The first and only time I fell in love I did not know about boundaries and balance. And perhaps I was on the other end of Luke's story. For four years I was getting my heart broken over and over until one day I had to break Alvin's heart. At first when Alvin did something that hurt my feelings, I would confront him, but it always started an altercation, and that made me feel worse. Eventually I hated confronting him about anything, so I stopped. I was afraid to speak my mind. Every time he upset me by changing our plans without telling me or breaking a promise, I accepted it and just turned the other cheek. I learned to love a man for the first time; however, it was an emotion that led me to lose too much of myself. Perhaps because I was so young, I did not know how to stop loving him. I did not know how to leave. After I graduated high school, the next two years of our encounters were centered by tumultuous instability. He would always come in and out of my life, because he knew I had not stopped loving him. One random day after three months of not hearing from him, he called me with the ultimate realization.

"Hello." I answered the phone.

"Hey, how are you?"

"Alvin?" I said.

"Yeah, it's me."

"I'm doing okay," I responded.

"I miss you. I know it's been a while," he said.

"Yeah, it has."

"Don't you miss me?" he asked.

There was a silent pause, and then I answered, "You were mean to me sometimes, and I don't miss that."

"I knew it was gonna be hard to get you back. I have been thinking about you so much. I want to read something to you." I heard him crackling paper that followed by my own words. "'I miss you so much when we aren't together. I love you so much and I know I always will. I know no one will ever change the way I feel about you.' You know who wrote that? You," he said.

I felt a sense of guilt. I had written him so many love letters in the four years that I was in love with him. I never pictured him keeping them as a reminder, as bait, holding a letter in front of me like some signed contract that I had no right to break. But that day I broke it; I broke his heart, and that was the last time I heard from him. I probably still loved him at the time, but at that moment I felt this sense of strength and courage that was telling me it was time to let go.

I also told him about my most recent relationship that lasted several months because it was a long-distance relationship with a guy that I had met in Mexico on one of my sanctuary getaways. He lived in Sayula, and his name was Daniel. Daniel was the brother of a girl to whom my brother, Angel, who passed away, was really close. Our relationship did not end too well for me, either. Perhaps it was my fault, because I never opened up and let him inside to get to know who I was and how I felt about him, the aftermath of my previous relationship. I became the kind of girl that sat there looking pretty and never said a word.

I did not let on that I had opinions and dreams. Within my culture, it was not acceptable for a female to be more goal oriented and ambitious than a man, much less her man—or, should I say, the "man to whom she belonged." I was more attentive to him and appeared to be low maintenance, especially when it came to expressing my feelings of discontent. I listened to his life stories about growing up poor before his family established their businesses, how he witnessed his father abuse his mother and then watched her suffer and eventually die due to breast cancer. Yet I bet he could not tell you whether or not I had brown or hazel eyes or what I wanted to be "when I grew up." I cared about him though, for a number of reasons. Mainly because his family was very accepting of me and I felt a part of something, which was a feeling that I struggled with in my own family at times. Although we only spent a summer together, Daniel and I had created so many memories that would allow me to fall in love with his soul. He spoke of marriage with me, but at this young age, marriage was just a "far, far away" fantasy. Four months later when I went back to Sayula for Christmas, he was happy to see me and continued to spend time with me until I saw him with another girl. I was in the town square with my friend Hannah, and there he was, opening his car door for some girl, and I walked up to him.

"Hey, I stopped by your house today. You know, to see your sister. You weren't there, though. I just wanted to say hi," I told him.

"Yeah," he responded nervously, but I was not the type to cause a big dramatic scene. "I went up to the mountains."

"That's what your dad said."

"Yeah, he's right," Daniel said.

"All right, well, I guess I'll see you around. It was good seeing you," I said walking away.

The next day he came to my house. In my experience, I have realized that men only recognize about twenty percent of their mistakes for which they are willing to apologize, and when they do, it is the only time it seems sincere.

"How are you?" Daniel asked.

"I was pretty upset, but I am better now. Besides, I didn't think you cared," I said.

"I do care," he responded matter-of-factly.

"Yeah, I see how much."

"Look, you were gone for four months. I didn't do anything wrong."

"Oh, and you couldn't have told me that you were already dating someone else when I got here, instead of stringing me along like nothing had changed?" I asked.

"It wasn't that easy. You know how I felt the day you surprised me at my house when you were back in town? I was so happy to see you. I felt like this sense of completeness seeing your face. I missed you. I knew you were only going to be here for a few days—"

I interrupted his statement, "and you figured you could just continue lying to me until I was gone again?"

"That's not fair!" He responded defensively and continued, "I wanted to enjoy these days with you. When you were here in the summer, I spent every day with you. I was so into you that there was no one else, the whole time I was with you. I do care about you, but you are the one that left me! You're not here! What do you expect me to do?"

I suppose I had no answer for that. Maybe what I expected was too much. The few times I had seen him in town after that we acted like strangers. The fact that he chose not to wait for me allowed me to understand that perhaps he did not love me like he wanted me to believe or like I wanted to be loved, a journey that would take me well into my years with many travelers.

It was not quite a full year after this break-up with Daniel when Luke was in the picture, but I did want to give romance another chance. I prayed to God that I could find a man who would accept me for the ambitious, outspoken female that I am; someone who would not only encourage and support me for it, but who would admire and challenge me in accomplishing my goals. It was pretty obvious that Luke and I were both into each other. However, we had both agreed that we wanted to take it slow because of our past relationships. His last relationship left the responsibility of a little boy. My last few relationships just left me with a broken heart, a shattered spirit, and a low capacity to believe that I could be loved. At the naïve age of twenty-one, I believed it when he said he did not want to hurt me; I also did not want him to hurt me. However, when he said he was having such overwhelming feelings that he should not be having, I realized that he was just as afraid of getting hurt as he was of hurting me, or perhaps he was still hurting. It did feel like our level of comfort and security was abnormally high that early on in our relationship, despite the fact that we were both so afraid of love.

We shared our future goals as well. Although at the time I was presently attending community college, I was working toward a future in journalism and writing, possibly one day having a PhD, teaching at a university, publishing poetry, and some day having a home in Mexico where I was happy and at peace. School, however, was part time until I could scrape together enough credits to transfer to a four-year university. I worked full time as a teacher's aide in a classroom of special needs children. Luke worked for a packaging/shipping service and cared for his little boy on the weekends. His future goals were a simpler life. He wanted to be happy, take care of his son, watch him grow, go back to school to get his GED, and maybe travel the world. We admired each other's goals. He was encouraging and wanted to see me continue to work hard toward all that I wanted, and I encouraged him to do the same.

After that conversation, I felt that God had answered my prayer to find a man that would be a positive influence on me in terms of recognizing and encouraging the ambition I possessed. Maybe Luke was not as ambitious as I was, but at least he still supported me. Luke was special and what I needed at the time. I was very much taken by the fact that I overwhelmed him immensely. He was intrigued by my personality, the way I dressed, the way I laughed, my smile, my spirit, my ambition. I was also convinced that although Luke was attracted to me, a small frame with long, curly black hair and a soft, copper-olive complexion, it was not the only reason why he had chosen to get to know me.

We spent many days getting to know each other on the phone before we got together again. Since we had unleashed the secrets of our past and our pathways toward the future, we focused on the present, what kind of a day we had, details of our daily activities, did we miss each other, and what in our day reminded us of the other. It was two weeks before we saw each other again. He was slowly learning about who I was from both our phone conversations and the comments from his friends that knew me. The more he learned about me, the more he was "afraid to hurt me." All he would ever tell me was the advice of our mutual friend, James. "That's not someone you want to hurt. She's a good girl." His apprehension about hurting me worried me. He would rave on and on about how special he thought I was. He made me feel appreciated for more than the way I looked. He made me feel like I could never disappoint him by just being myself, but why so much energy placed on the thought of hurting me?

Our next encounter was by mistake. Our lives' schedules always conflicted. We both worked, I was in school, and he had his son. I had invited him to a party my sister's boyfriend was having. Luke said that he was not able to go, because he was going to have his son that night. I understood and went to the party without him. After the party we went to Twister's, the local club. I excused myself to the restroom, and there he was, at the bar's entrance. He looked at me very surprised, as if he was happy to see me. I, on the other hand, felt the taste of dissension in my throat, but it was at that moment that I had finally understood what he meant when he said he was afraid of hurting me.

He stopped me and said, "Gimme me a hug!"

I had just pushed right through the crowd to the restroom, indicating that it was an emergency so as not to appear rude or upset. I was not sure how to feel. Of course I was happy to see him; however, I was hurt and confused at what appeared to be a lie. I also wondered how he even got in the club. On my way back from the restroom I saw him at the bar holding an empty stool for me, so I went and sat in it.

"Why didn't you give me a hug? How are you? Here, sit down." He was still holding out the stool for me, and as I sat down he gave me a hug. I merely patted him on the back.

"I'm good," I responded. "What are you doing here? I thought you couldn't go out because you were watching your son."

He was so nonchalant the way he spoke to me, perhaps it was just me over reacting. "He fell asleep early. The guys called me to go out for a drink, and my mom said she would keep an eye on him in case he woke up. Just relax. Come on, have a drink with me. How was the party?" He hailed over the bartender and ordered two beers.

"It was all right." Out of mere curiosity, I had to ask, "How did you get in here, anyway?"

"I know the bouncer," he said.

Our conversation eventually moved from the party to how his week went, to how work was going for me and about his son. We spent an hour together talking, and then I had to leave. He called me when he got home at four in the morning. He said he was not tired and wanted to talk, but yet he ended up falling asleep on the phone.

A few days later he called and asked me to spend Saturday evening with him.

"So, I need to see you again," Luke said.

"What did you have in mind?" I asked.

"I am sitting for a friend. He went out of town. I want you to come by."

"For what?" I said with a curious smile.

"A tantalizing dinner, some interesting conversation, and some delicious kisses that you owe me," was his charming response.

"How can I say no to that interesting menu?" I said.

It was the first time that we were alone. I was nervous because I wondered if every moment we shared together would be like the first. I know now that the first mistake I made was holding this relationship's expectations to the magic and fantasy of that first night. Another reason why I was nervous to be alone with him was because I was going through a spiritual cleansing of abstaining from sex. Judith and I made a pact to show reverence to God. We were in the process of trying to get closer to Him, trying to have a better relationship with Him. Judith and I had been hurt in relationships too often. We knew only God could give us what we were looking for and what we needed. Although Alvin and I did make a physical connection, I did not make the same mistake with Daniel. Judith's sister, who was only a year older than us, got pregnant about two years ago. The thought of pregnancy scared us into abstinence, and for me, it had been in effect almost two years. So it was a decision that I made to make me a stronger person and more spiritually connected to God. We had gone to confession and freed ourselves of guilt and disconnection from God through absolution.

Luke made the most of entertaining me at his friend's house. He had a dinner ready for me. It was a simple dish of pasta, jarred marinara sauce, and Caesar salad, and to drink he had Bacardi lime with sprite, and I drank water. We talked and laughed most of the night. He had an amazing sense of humor and a delicate way of choosing his words and delivering his stories. We eventually moved our conversation to the couch where he wanted me to watch his favorite movie, *Braveheart*. It would be a movie that we would attempt to watch many times, but I have yet to see it in its entirety. There were times that night when we would get carried away by our passions, but Luke was very respectful and knew when to slow down. He withdrew a sense of guilt in me, but I was not sure if it was because I had offended him or God. He was patient with me. I felt as if I had been involved with this man for years. Before I knew it, the sun had risen. I felt awkward in this new territory, because even though I maintained my abstinence, I had never before watched the sunrise with a man.

He called me a few days later, already having my schedule memorized. Knowing that I had class Tuesday evenings, he called when I was getting in bed. I told him I wanted to take this relationship slow and control my emotions, but they pretty much had a mind of their own. He understood exactly what I meant. It felt as though our feelings were trying to rush into a relationship, but our thoughts knew to be logical.

The next several weeks we began to make plans where we would involve each other and accommodate each other, but I wondered if we could be somewhere together where he would not need a drink.

Unfortunately, most of our weekend plans were showing up at the same parties, clubs, or local events. Although we would not go together, we would be at the same place at the same time. I would show up with my friends, and he would show up with his. I liked to mingle, and so did he. Even though we were not at each other's side, we were both aware of each other. Once in a while we would dance together. Every now and then one of us would check in on the other replenishing each other's drinks or accompanying each other on trips to the restroom. On occasion we would just want a hug or kiss from each other and talk for a bit. Sometimes we would leave together, and other times we left separately, but at the same time. In which case he would call me when he got home and tell me all the thoughts and fun he had that night. Mostly he would tell me how beautiful he thought I was, or the funny little quirks I did or said, or how much I made him smile. It was not as easy for me to compliment him. I tended to keep in any positive emotion, because I did not want to reveal any sign of weakness and vulnerability. I do not know if he ever knew how much I liked him, how attractive I thought he was, or how intelligent and interesting I thought he was. I just know that I ate up his compliments but cheated him out of his share.

I also began to feel the tension and hostility that existed between him and his son's mother when he talked about her. There were occasions when we would be on the phone and she would show up to pick up or drop off their son. Sometimes it was unexpected and so he would have to call me back. He would tell me how much he hated her. Other times he would not have to tell me, because I could hear the hostile way he spoke to her and the contempt in his voice, and how he objected to her ways of parenting their son.

"What are you doing here now?" Luke asked her.

"I want my son." She sounded so blasé, as though the existing rules and boundaries did not apply to her.

"He's asleep. You're supposed to come tomorrow. I'm not waking him up," he said.

"Well, I forgot I had to take him to my cousin's baby's birthday party," she informed him.

"Well, why can't you just get him in the morning?" Luke asked.

"I don't want to get up early," she replied.

"Well, too bad. I'm not waking him up." I could hear the frustration in Luke's voice.

"Then I'm not bringing him next weekend," she said. It was around this time that he would "have to call me back." These were the times that he was at his worst. His son was his life, and without him he could not breathe. I never knew any of the details about Luke and his son's mother, but I wondered if I did, would it be something that would hurt me. Why did he have so much hostility toward her still? I could not help but replay in my mind his comment, "*I broke her heart, and then she broke mine.*" Was he still heart broken and blaming her?

One cool, crisp, winter December night Luke and I walked home from a party around the corner from his house. He led me by the hand on the way to his home, trying to keep me warm. I was mesmerized by his gentility. I admired the quality of sensitivity that he possessed. We sat on his porch and talked and kissed. We gazed at the stars and breathed in the cool air, during all the while I felt like something from a dream or fairy tale. He introduced me to his sister and her husband. She told me that I was pretty. I was inching my way to a new level of comfort, and I was just letting it happen. I was not fighting the feeling that I had been afraid to feel for the past couple of years.

Luke lived in the basement of his parents' home. It was very basic. He slept on a pullout couch with a television directly placed in front of it. The basement was a place for him to relax. He went in to the restroom and I sat on the bed, waiting. He came out dressed in something more comfortable. Then I went into the restroom to freshen up. When I came out, he was lying down, and he had turned off the light.

"Where are you, I can't see you." I knew he was exaggerating because the street light peeked into the window.

"You can see me," I said.

"I can't, but I can always tell when you're smiling. I can hear it in your voice. I love that about you. Come lay down with me. Are you tired?" Luke inquired.

"A little. Why?" I lay down next to him feeling a little uncomfortable. This was not like the first time I spent the night when I knew I had control. He placed the blanket on top of me and felt around to ensure that every inch of my body was covered and then he placed his hand on my shoulder. I lay with my back to him, too afraid to face him directly.

"Maybe you wanna talk. Did you have fun?" Luke asked.

I laughed, thinking back to a funny moment we had shared, "Yeah, I did."

"Are you thinking about that drink you dropped on that guy's head. That was pretty funny," he said teasingly.

"It wasn't my fault. Someone bumped me," I said.

"You got freaked out when he told you that you had to kiss him or he'd kick you out," he said.

"Did you hear him say that? Because you came to my rescue right away."

"I'm always watching you out of the corner of my eye, making sure you don't cause any trouble." Luke said, still teasing me.

"Trouble?" I repeated.

He laughed. He had admitted that night at the party that I was with him. He came to my rescue and asked the host if he had met "his girl."

"Yeah, Wayne thought you were pretty cute. He wouldn't have kicked you out," he said.

Luke began to kiss me and touch me, and I turned to face him. The dark warmth of his arms consumed me, not to be dissolved until the next morning, leaving me with a feeling of satisfaction, tempered by regret. I felt confused and a little disappointed in myself. I had broken my bond with God, and we were now disconnected. It might not have seemed like a big deal to most people, but I tried to live my life as though God watched every minute of it.

Luke was the only guy that could get me to do the craziest things that I would have never imagined myself doing. He would get me to spend more nights to watch more sunrises with him. In conversation we shared our different music interests and talked about literature and spirituality. I introduced the music of Shakira to him before she went American mainstream and the political music of Molotov, and he shared with me the talent of Billie Holiday. Whenever I spent the night, I never fell asleep. I lay there awake as he slept. Sometimes I would read the books he had lying around. He had a great sense of literature that he alone developed and honed, Spanish Golden Age drama, Romanticism, and American Modern poetry. I did not know what our relationship was exactly, but nonetheless, it was happening. He had never asked me for a commitment or to be exclusive. I was always too afraid to ask questions about our relationship. In the first place, I did not want to know the truth. I was also afraid of how he would react. We went on with our relationship like this a little longer before it began to change.

By the end of January we spent less and less time on the phone. I sensed the drug that I once was for him begin to wear off, and his own reality was creeping up on him again. School and work kept me busy at times, and I was not always able to make him feel the stimulating satisfaction that I had initially, and so he needed to find something else that would. I felt as though he was losing interest in me, and so I decided to date other people. He obviously was not looking for a relationship, and I was not even sure what I wanted. I still had feelings for him, but I was getting so much attention from other men that I wanted to explore those options. Unfortunately, I really liked Luke, and although we did not want the same thing, I did not want to let him go. The other men I dated were attractive and kind, but their personalities did not keep me drawn to them. Talking to them was boring. They had no passions in life or ambitions that would move them forward. I even noticed how much more intelligent Luke was than most other men our age. It was not a book smart he possessed, it was an intuition or sixth sense about life and spirituality. He also knew how to be in tune with a woman. He was sensitive and not afraid to show that he had feelings. On the contrary, I was the one afraid to show my feelings. I was so removed emotionally that he did not know how I felt, because I never expressed my emotions. In his frustrated manner he would manage to let me know how he felt, and it forced me to have to talk about my feelings.

"Why don't you ever say what you feel?" Luke asked me. "I hate that about you. I tell you how much I like you. I wish I knew what was going on inside of you."

"I like you, too. If I didn't, I wouldn't be trying to spend time with you. I thought that was enough. Do I have to say it? I like you. I like talking to you. I think you're smart," I said.

I watched a smile form on his face, a satisfaction he received when getting me to open up in a hostile way. "I think you're beautiful," he said victoriously.

By February our relationship had come to an end. There were fewer and fewer conversations and plans. There was a casual phone call once a week, and eventually that phone call no longer made its way. Regardless of where we were within our relationship, all that had mattered to me was focusing on school. This was the year that I would transfer to a four-year university and be that much closer to one of my goals. I was in the last semester of completing my associate's degree and ensuring that I met all the graduation requirements.

Luke had called me one day out of the blue and informed me of a party he was having with his friends. When I arrived, I saw that I was merely an invited guest. He was acting as bartender and carrying on every now and again with friends as well as other girls. I realized that it was the end of our relationship, and I wondered if we would still maintain a friendship. I knew that Luke and I had the same fear, fear of a broken heart. On the bright side, I had the memory of Luke's smile. I tried my hardest to just leave this ending in God's hands.

Your Smile

In a gust of wind you were left behind,
without a thought of what you would find.
Considering in a sense you had lost a little hope.
You changed your priorities and turned to God to cope.

So when a sensational feeling took you by surprise,
your heart and your mind made a compromise.
You did not fall and you did not fly.
You solely trusted the tone in your sigh.

In just one kiss you felt the faith and honesty.
You were swiftly taken by appearance and personality.
Within a short time it was a blessing too good to be true.
Your one doubt was caused by the past you went through.

But when you replay in your mind the present memories,
a smile occurs and you get weak in the knees.
At every sight and sound and thought and touch,
your smile continues to develop so much.
So if you are afraid or unsure, then just take it slow
and remember that it's your smile that will always know.

To recover from my temptations with Luke, I sought absolution. Confession is the best action I can take for cleansing my soul. Priests are an instrument of God. When I confess to them, I hear God's voice and wisdom. I see His forgiving and compassionate face. I feel relieved and motivated. I know that I am ready to move forward and leave my mistakes behind.

I knew part of trying to live a life with God meant that I had to stay away from Luke. I avoided calling him and hoped he would not call me. I wanted to restore my emotional and spiritual connection with God and with the people that did matter to me. In Sayula, March was a glorious time of celebration, and it was what I needed to forget about Luke. I arranged a week away from work and school and went to the carnival in Sayula, to find my spiritual peace.

JACOB, THE FLOOD, AND EDEN

Then the Lord planted a garden in Eden, in the East...
Out of the ground the Lord God made various trees grow
that were delightful to look at and good for food, with the
tree of life in the middle of the garden and the tree of the
knowledge of good and bad.

Genesis 2:8-9

Sayula is a small town, population thirty thousand, or maybe even less. It has grown since I was first brought here; it is not like it used to be. Until I got older, the only perimeters I ever knew in Sayula were the *colonia* in which my grandparents lived when I was growing up and a few other colonies that surrounded it. My grandfather had many properties throughout the town in each of the four corners; that is how I learned how big it actually was for a small town.

One of my closest friends in Sayula was Hannah. She was dark skinned and thick bodied. I had known her and her family since I was four or five. Hannah was a home body; it was like pulling teeth to get her to go out with me. She preferred spending time at home with family or friends. She was open-minded, and for some reason, wise, maybe from staying home and watching all those *novelas*. Hannah was with me when I saw Daniel with that other girl. It seemed as though she always knew the right thing to say to me to make me feel better, like she did get advice from a soap opera. I cannot remember the day I met her, but what I do remember is that we have always been friends. Especially when there came a time when the older I got the less other girls of the *pueblo* wanted to be my friend. Not only was I close to Hannah, but having known her for so long, and our fathers having grown up at the same time, in the same place, I was close to her family. I had my first kiss with one of her brothers and a sincere secret crush on another. It was the summer after my freshman year of high school. It was another summer visit to Sayula to see my grandparents.

I was fourteen when I had my first kiss. I felt as though I was kind of older than the average young lady, but intimacy with boys did not interest me that much. Even then, I was not very impressed or emotionally moved by the kiss. Hannah had a brother, two years older than me, Noah, and a brother two years younger than me, Jacob. I had to assume Noah was more experienced with the opposite sex than I was, because at the time I had very little experience with boys. What intrigued me about Noah was not so much whether I liked him, or that he was cute and he was older, but it was the fact that he showed interest in me, and it was flattering because I grew up in the shadow of an older, "prettier" sister. I always had to hear about how pretty Phoebe was, or how skinny she was. I felt as though someone was actually looking at me and finally telling me that I was pretty too, and that I deserved attention. Since our vacation time never lasted more than ten days, I looked forward to the evenings where I would meet Noah at his older sister's house. And when he was at his sister's house we would talk while he did his homework, since Mexico's school sessions ran longer than ours did, or he would study for his entrance exam to get into military school. I did not know what to say except smile and thank him for all the compliments he gave me. I was nervous around him, unsure of what to say, how to act or even of what the right feeling was that I was supposed to feel. He would tell me that I was pretty and ask me about boyfriends that I may have had. To seem confident I acted like I knew I was pretty, but I felt insecure about the way I looked. Since I was never the one to get the praise of beauty, I did not know if I believed it.

During the day, there were times when I would be next door at Hannah's sister's house and I would run into Jacob, the younger brother. He had three sides to him that I got to know a little that summer. He was funny; he made me laugh; more importantly, he made me smile. His smile was very contagious. It was a very toothy grin with a tinge of mischief. He had a raw, sometimes harmful sense of humor where he played mean tricks on people and made fun of people in order to get a laugh. I felt honored at never having been a subject of his cruel humor. Even when he was not being cruel to get laughs, he had a fun side to him. He liked to laugh and have fun and make other people laugh as well. On other occasions I caught him having arguments with his sisters or the neighborhood kids, and I could tell he had a very vengeful and heartless streak in him when someone hurt, shamed, or insulted him. He was the type of person that would never walk away from a fight and would rarely ever lose a fight. And in one particular instance, I discovered what I would consider for a person like him, his flirty side, or maybe it was his intimate-sensitive side. This was the side that as he got older not very many people would ever get to witness.

The family owned a store, and the area behind their older sister's house was what they used as a storage room. Jacob peeked through the curtain window and saw me sitting there alone. He only showed one eye. "Have you seen my sister?" Jacob asked.

"She went to the *centro*; I'm just waiting for her to come back. She shouldn't be too much longer," I responded.

"Who else is with you?" he continued to inquire.

"No one, just me," I said.

"So you're alone?"

"Yeah, I guess," I said. This was his cue to reveal the rest of his face from behind the curtain. "How are you? I like your clothes, the way you dress. You look nice. You're pretty, and just right. Your sister is too skinny. I don't like that," Jacob said eagerly. At that time, and with an older-sister-shadowed self-esteem, I found it flattering. I should have just taken it as a compliment, but at that age, I took it that he liked me. It was what I wanted to believe, because I believed it was the way I felt about him. More than anything he made me laugh and appreciated the way I looked. He was able to look past my sister and see me.

That summer not only did I look forward to my evenings with Noah, but what I mostly looked forward to each day were my random run-ins with Jacob, any time and any place. Sometimes we would talk for five seconds, and sometimes for hours, but they were all like shots of espresso to me. He made me giddy. He would ask me what life was like in Chicago. Although I lived in a small city outside of Chicago, no one would know what I was talking about unless I just said Chicago. I could not even tell them I lived in Illinois, because geographically, Chicago was more known to people in small towns of Mexico than the state in which it resided. Although I liked Jacob more, I continued my evening visits with Noah. I know I was just humoring him, making him believe that I liked him only because I liked the attention.

The night before I returned home, I gave Noah one of my school pictures, and he kissed me for the first time, "like a grown up." My family always headed out of Sayula at midnight to make the Sierra Madre Occidental Mountains by morning. So the next morning when I awoke to the spiral of a vehicular turn, I laid there on the floor behind the first seat of our van, reflecting on my first kiss. It was nice, but I began to think that it was not as special as I would have imagined my first kiss. I could not help but think about Jacob and our *adieu*. It was pretty basic and simple, but it was just as emotionally moving as my first kiss.

"You leaving today?" Jacob asked.

"Yes," I responded. Not really knowing what to feel.

"Well, you and your family have a safe trip. Take care. I guess I'll see you next year," he said and shook my hand. I thanked him. Those were the memories and emotions I was left with of the two.

March was Sayula's carnival time. Every day and every night spectacular events occurred: rodeo shows, concerts from well-known bands, parades, a carnival of rides, and many dances and parties. It all lasted a week long and then it moved on to the next town. I arrived on a Saturday morning. Hannah and her older sister had picked me up at the Miguel Hidalgo International Airport in Guadalajara, an hour and a half from the *pueblo*. After a few hours of catching up on sleep due to jet lag, I was ready to enjoy the festivities. In the afternoon was the big parade where kids, teens, and church volunteers dressed in native attire performed a number of traditional dances and marches as they walked. Businesses advertised their services, and the *pueblo's* queen candidates paraded on brightly colored decorated floats and automobiles to influence votes for becoming Sayula's next queen. Later that night Banda Recodo performed.

The whole week I focused on enjoying myself. At night, I went to dances and bull fights and parties and rejoiced with my friends. In the day I would watch the parades or go visit my grandmother. She would send me on errands buying groceries or collecting the rent from her properties. She no longer lived in the house by Hannah's sister. After my grandfather had passed, my grandmother moved into a different home that contained less asbestos. Upon her request, I would go and visit her friends from the old neighborhood to tell them that she was doing well. The house in which we used to live was now a small *tortilla* factory. Hannah's aunt lived on the other side of my grandparent's property and my grandmother was good friends with her. She was never there when I went, but her son David usually was. He was about seventeen or eighteen and very pale complexioned.

"Hi, Little David." Even though he was not so little anymore, I had just gotten into the habit of calling him Little David, pretty much since he was two or so. It seemed like it was part of his name, his identity. "Is your mom around?" I asked.

"No, she is out, the *centro* somewhere," David said.

"My *abuelita* sent me over, can you let her know to call her or something," I said

"Yeah. Hey, can I ask you something?" said David.

"Sure," I replied.

"What's the north like? I mean I'm heading out there, and I just want to know what it's like, what to expect," David inquired. Mexicans always referred to the United States as "the North."

"I don't know. It's like any other place, I guess. What are you gonna be doing over there?" I asked out of curiosity.

"Well, Jacob and Noah are out there. They said they would help me get a job and I can stay with them," he responded.

"Jacob? So you're going to California? What's the matter, you don't like it here anymore? Your mom can't be happy about this."

"It's just something I have to do, you know, leave. Start new, start over," he said with reluctance.

"Is something wrong?" I asked

"Uh…no, not really," David said hesitantly.

"Oh, well good luck, I guess," I said.

I was not sure what to say about what life is like in America. People do not realize that it might be a different experience for people like me and my family. Although not all of my family members were born in the country, we were all raised in the country except for my father. Although we might be considered first generation Mexican-American, we took advantage of our opportunities to get educated. I do not think it would be the same kind of experience for David: undocumented, uneducated, and unfamiliar with the language. It is not until the next generation or two when families can begin to benefit from the privileged life of America, and that is only if they take advantage of it. It was pretty typical that around his age many boys illegally immigrate to the United States. They try to avoid required military service at eighteen or they want the opportunity to make "American dollars" to send back to their families. Sometimes it was the first alternative to avoid run-ins with the law, like for both Daniel and Jacob.

Throughout the day what I tried not to do was think about Luke. In fact, I had run into Daniel's sister. Daniel and his family were also special to me, because they knew my brother, the one that had passed away. His sister dated Angel and they had remained very good friends after their break-up. She was pretty surprised to see me. Usually I was in town only in the summertime or on occasion Christmas time, but never in March. Perhaps it was not that much of a coincidence that we ran into each other. I had slipped out late at night from Hannah's house to sit on Daniel's porch. Instead of dwelling on Luke, I began to think about Daniel. Daniel no longer lived in the town due to some trouble he made for himself. He was gone, already "in the north." From what I was told, he got into a fight outside the bullfighting stadium and stabbed a guy who eventually bled to death. He was arrested later that night for murder, but three months later his cell was empty. He and a few other prisoners managed to escape and were now somewhere in California. Although I was not with Daniel for very long, our relationship was still very special to me. I was with Daniel during my abstinence period, and so our relationship meant a lot to me because of the respect he had for me. Due to my relationship with Alvin, I had a healthier outer self-esteem than inner. I knew I was pretty now, but I was no longer confident in letting guys know I was opinionated, ambitious, and intelligent, so I had let Daniel use me as a trophy.

There was this intense view of the mountains if you sat in the right spot of the porch. Daniel and I spent a lot of our time sharing this view together. I stared at the beautiful scene that became a screen where I could replay the sweet moments we had shared—and even the anticipated moments we had not. I looked around like a movie camera imagining Daniel and myself in our roles, sometimes rewriting the ending.

My last night in Sayula, Hannah and I went to the little dance hall, *el disco*. The waiter, Alejandro, was very attentive to us. Granted, Hannah and I were practically the only people in the place. We just wanted to play some pool and have a calm evening of catching up on our lives before I returned to Illinois. She was a good listener and a nonjudgmental person. We had fun even though it was a mellow night. Because business was slow, Alejandro was able to play a few games with us.

He asked me a lot of questions about what I liked to do, and especially about school. "So what are you studying in school?"

"Journalism," I said.

"What kind of things do you write about?" Alejandro asked me.

"It depends, mostly news, but I like to do viewpoint pieces about what affects the Latino population on campus and within our communities," I responded.

"Really? Me too. I'm in school to be a lawyer. I also focus on the politics of Mexico and how all these politicians take advantage of the poor people. I want to be the one that helps them. What type of injustices do you see?" he asked.

"Well, I don't know if I would say I write about injustices, but more of informing the population of what their rights are. There wouldn't be so many unjust actions if people knew what they had a right to," I said.

"I guess the contrary here is that when people try to exercise their rights, they are treated even more unfairly." This was mostly the topic of conversation we had through all the shooting and breaking of the pool balls. Aside from being a nice guy, he was intelligent and ambitious. He had a light complexion that contrasted well with his dark wavy hair. Like most of my male counterparts, he was short, but taller than me. He was fit, physically. He had somewhat of a rough look about him in his face when he was not smiling. Getting to know Alejandro was the end of my time in Mexico away from my life in Illinois.

Once I returned from Mexico I needed time to myself. I was in a place where I did not know what I wanted, except to finish school and be able to continue moving forward toward my plan with God. If anything, when it came to relationships, I did not know what I was doing. I had to trust that God knew what was in store for me, and I had to focus on school. For the next couple of months I did not talk to Luke or date any one else. I did not want to be in a vulnerable state and around charismatic men that would recognize my weakness and prey on me. I needed to settle a lot of emotions that were doing me more harm than good. I spent time with friends and tutoring people. It always made me feel good to recognize the talents and gifts that God gave me and share them with others. It was important to me to serve others in the name of the Lord.

It was also around this time that I started to feel a sense of how much I wanted to get out of my sad, gloomy, little town. I received a letter from a good friend in the military I had known since grade school who told me she was deployed to Germany and how she was visiting places like France and Italy. I thought, not that I had a desire to go to Europe, but I just knew that one day I wanted out of this cage in which I was raised, a place where I felt I no longer belonged and that God must have something more for me. In the same week I ran into a friend from middle school who told me how he was modeling in New York, Europe, and Los Angeles and I began to wonder when it would be my turn to escape. I had shared my thoughts and encounters with Judith, and she told me, "When you have the opportunity to get out of here, you have to take it, otherwise you'll be stuck here forever!"

I suffocated at the thought of having to stay here forever and grew emptier. I used to believe that my future lay in the hands of a man. That he would be an excuse to run away, but there is no freedom in changing from one cage to another. I was tired of feeling trapped, by my environment, by my family, by my emotions, by the power I gave men over me. I took these encounters as a sign from God that I had to refocus my priorities and not lose sight of my goals, because if I did, I would lose sight of His plan. I did not know yet what that plan was, but I knew that it required for me to keep going to school. It was pertinent for me to finish. After a few days of fearful hopelessness, I was empowered by the Holy Trinity to reach deep inside and pull out all the strength and courage for which I had ever prayed, all the patience with which I had been blessed, and most importantly, all the reverence that the Holy Spirit had given me as a significant gift that would not allow any other human being come between us, in order to accomplish His greater plan that would one day rescue me from this environment. I eagerly hoped for God to show me an escape on His time.

It was not that our environment was that bad, but more of what surrounded it, racism, gang activity and violence, teenage pregnancy, and eventually, lost hopes. What surrounded me was so discouraging. I had set my hopes on one school only after community college. As I waited for a reply from Saint Ambrose University, I imagined it as a ticket forward, closer physically to removing myself from what I was already disconnected emotionally. I isolated myself from what I did not want to be a part. I wanted to leave this little town. Even though this university is only forty-five minutes from my home, I would live on campus or closer to the school, farther away from the trap in which I lived. I know now that I should not have confused reverence with isolation, but I was in a different place than most people I knew. Friends my age or younger were already parents who put their dreams on hold, or stuck in some unfulfilling job; they had already buried their dreams and goals. I felt successful in isolation, proud of the grades I was receiving in school, proud that during the second week of April the letter arrived in the mail accepting me into Saint Ambrose University. I was beginning to taste accomplishment, and it was definitely a satisfying dish that I would continue to crave throughout my life, so long as I knew that nothing would ever come between God and me. For the next couple of months, the thought of being able to leave Piano City motivated me. Getting accepted into this university was one of the greatest blessings that I could have been given at this time.

When I shared this blessing with my family, they did not share my enthusiasm. I knew it would be a challenge because, despite my age, within my culture it was not common for a father to let his young, single daughter stray far from the nest. But I remembered what God wanted, and I had to continue to follow the fact that I could not allow anyone between us and that reverence and courage were given to me by the Holy Spirit; I needed to use these gifts, especially to have the strength to tolerate my family's reaction.

"That's a private school, right? Isn't that gonna cost a lot of money," said my brother, Joseph, as if he would be the one footing the bill.

"That's nice," was my sister, Phoebe's response.

"So what does this mean?" my mother asked.

"What do you mean? We talked about this. We made a deal: if I pay for the first half of my education, you would help me when I was ready to transfer," I replied.

"Well, wasn't that a few years ago," she continued.

"I guess, but I still did it. You should be happy for me," I said.

"We are; your father and I are happy for you," said my mother.

"I think under the circumstances it might be best if I lived on campus," I informed my parents.

"We never discussed that," she replied with surprise.

"Well, do it now," I suggested.

"Your father and I need some time to discuss it," she said.

"Fine," I haughtily responded. My mother always had to be the one to express both her and my father's feelings.

I do not know why they wasted their time looking like there was a possibility of telling me no. They knew that when I was determined to accomplish something, they couldn't stop me. Although I felt punches of discouragement from my family at times, I had to remember that God would give me all the support I needed. Nevertheless, I did not realize how deep the lack of support from the people I loved scarred my soul. God gave me strength so I could continue to move forward, alone, if necessary, so long as I continued to follow Him.

People's lack of support only pushed me to set more goals and follow through. Although I no longer shared the dreams and goals that existed in my head, it did not cause me to stop dreaming. I began to create this world in my mind where I was accomplishing all my deepest desires, and for once they were safe from people who would try to destroy them or take them away. I decided that for now I would just keep to myself, but when it was time to arrive at my new school, I would break my sense of isolation. Naturally, I set my new goals. I would continue to get involved with the school's newspaper and become a part of its Latino organization. Although I at times questioned my abilities, I knew that God did not. I took tours of the university, scheduled meetings with advisors, and I observed other students to understand what my new environment would be like, how different it would be compared to the one I wanted so desperately to leave behind. Perhaps the longings to be alone would start to change if I could make emotional and spiritual connections with meaningful people.

Close to the end of the semester and seizing the opportunity of a new environment, I decided to seek out Luke. I needed positive reinforcement. In addition to knowing that he would be proud of my accomplishment, without expressing any kind of doubt, I did not want to forget about the spiritual connection that we shared. I still wondered if we could possibly have some kind of future together. I wondered if we were still meeting a greater plan of God by continuing to share the same path on our journey. I wondered if our spiritual connection would be strong enough to sustain a friendship; was he spiritually connected enough to sustain me in order for me to no longer have to isolate myself? He was a good listener, and as long as I did not expect anything more, he would be a good friend.

He was happy to hear from me and pleased to hear of my news, as I knew he would be. We slowly continued to reestablish a friendship. He would call me when he needed to talk, and often times it was when he was alone and had a few drinks. He was always feeling alone. He would continue to gripe about his son's mother and bounce from job to job. I would tell him to hang in there or suggest actions he could take to make his situation better, but he did not want solutions from me. He wanted my compassion, or perhaps my pity. Once in a while he wanted my company, but I did not want to see him because I did not want to fall into temptation. I stayed away from him physically. We maintained a friendship by phone only. I spoke of my goals, shared poetry with him, and he would tell me what a talented writer he thought I was. I fed off his support and encouragement, since it was such a rare resource in my life. I continued to be on the other end of the phone as often as he wanted me to be. It was not a hard task, because he did not need me that often. He was safe for me, so long as I was not physically in his presence.

I waited for the time to pass, and in the second week of May, I finished my associate's degree. Eventually the summer came around and my parents planned their trip to Texas and Mexico. It was a peaceful time for me to be in Sayula. Friday nights were family dinner nights, but on the night of the trip, we never knew what would happen. Sometimes my father's job did not release him until late at night, and other times he got out of there exactly at five. I do not remember the process much when we were little, but I know my mother was the one that had to pack up her four kids and husband for a two-week vacation every summer. From the age that I do remember, I was the one that helped my sister pack, which was ironic, because she was much more organized than me. We were so obsessive about "the trip." We would always make lists: how much clothes to bring, socks? Shoes? Bottoms? Underwear? For how many days? What days would we spend driving, and what days would we be in Texas, and how many days in Mexico? When we got old enough, my mother was freed of the food shopping and packing. Every task was a treat when it came to "the trip." Everyone had their stations in the van, too. My parents were in the front, I had the middle passenger seat all to myself. Phoebe and Joseph shared the seat behind me, and Angel was in the back, in charge of the food and easy access to my dad in case there was any van trouble. Sometimes we switched spots for a while for different reasons. It had been this way for many years, until Angel passed away. Angel passed away when I was only seventeen, so the following year Joseph moved to the back.

Soon we would all be too old for this if people did not think we were already. After all, I was the youngest and already twenty-two years old. Every time we pulled into the little quiet town, I felt a whole different sense of self. I was viewed differently in the eyes of the town's people. I had a separate life, separate memories, a separate sense of peace. I felt like I was someone else, as though I could forget about my life in Illinois and live a fairy tale life for a few weeks, as if my life was perfect. People in the town had perceived this image of my family and me, and I fed into it. I was this spoiled little rich girl from America, beautiful and intelligent because I was influenced by American culture. I was supposedly dressed in the latest fashions and they were accompanied by the latest accessories. I was up with the latest music, movies, and movie stars, although, like most typical families, we shopped at both marts and basic department stores, places that were not special or expensive, but the people in Mexico did not know that. We were nowhere near rich, although some might say a little spoiled. We just had really great parents.

My cousin, brother, and sister wanted to go to *el disco* in town. It was the one where Alejandro worked. During that time it was the only one in Sayula. I looked forward to seeing Alejandro, because it was easy to be with him. He had no expectations of me. Unfortunately, it was not like the last time I was there. It was a Saturday night, and it was packed. Like any typical club, there were lots of people dancing, talking, drinking, and smoking. The music was loud and rhythmic. Alejandro would talk to me every now and then, but he was extremely busy. He was very attentive to my family. I was attracted to his hospitality and ambition of which I was informed the last time we were able to talk.

As we were leaving, he pulled me aside and asked, "Do you think you could come back tomorrow? I have to work, but you know how slow business is on Sundays. We could spend more time together. I really enjoy talking to you."

"I'm not sure. I think my family has plans for us," I responded.

"Well, what about Monday?" Alejandro asked.

"Maybe. I don't think we have anything planned," I said.

"Well, maybe I can go visit you at your grandma's house," he suggested.

"Okay."

"In the evening, around seven?" he asked.

I agreed and awaited his arrival at my home on Monday.

I liked Alejandro, but I had the constant reminder in my head that no one would come between me and God. I took the chance anyway to spend time with Alejandro outside of his work; unfortunately, when it came to my dad's family, whims occurred without a moment's notice. At the last minute they were always deciding to drive to Guayabitos, Talpa, the mountains, or Ciudad Guzman. He had come over to my house on Monday to find it empty. My father woke us all up at five in the morning to go to the mountains, the very mountains that Daniel and I admired together from his house. My father had a cousin who owned a ranch above our town. We would drive up the mountains and sit around just hearing my dad, his sisters, brothers, and cousins talk about their life growing up and their family adventures. They spoke of how natural it was to run around barefoot with sticks—their choice of childhood toys—chasing lizards, eating natural fruits from the trees, and feeling lost but yet at home within the huge grounds. I followed a butterfly's erratic path and envied its spirit. I sat on the ground and ate the sweet, red seeds of a pomegranate with God. They reminded me of rosary beads. Later I returned to my family and we ate *carne asada* and absorbed the nature of the trees and trails. It was peaceful and quiet. The smells were both natural and distinct to the setting. I liked it, despite the fact that I missed an anticipated encounter. It was not a bad moment with my family. We headed back home around midnight, and by then there was not much more to do but reflect and go to bed.

Upon my return from Mexico I felt nostalgic, as I did every time I left. I always felt like a new person when I returned from Mexico, emotionally, spiritually, mentally and physically rested. Everything was so different, and it caused me to see myself in a whole different perspective. I knew that I did not like where I had returned, so anywhere I went almost always caused a contrasting feeling. I wanted to break my cycle of isolation. So I tried to make efforts to go out with my friends and family. On the Fourth of July, Judith and I went to The Taste of Chicago, one of Chicago's biggest summer events. Anything could happen in Chicago on a night like July Fourth, but with Judith at my side I was safe from temptation. Ironically, I ran into James, Luke, and other high school buddies at the train station. I was not sure how to react to seeing Luke, but I could tell James was more excited to see me than Luke was. He always was. Although we grew up next door to each other, by junior high neither one of us lived in the same place. Anytime I saw him in the halls of high school, I felt safe and secure seeing his familiar face. He had always been protective of me, and I appreciated him for that. Luke, on the other hand, had a drink in one hand and was keeping his balance with the other. He hugged me, told me he was happy to see me, and that he would be calling me. I knew I should not have been so accepting and forgiving of him, but I had very little backbone. That was a characteristic I developed from my relationship with Alvin, fear of the truth.

When I think about the kind of man with whom I would like to share my future, I think of someone who sets high aspirations for himself. It would be someone extraordinary. It would

o sought God to change their life for the better
anything else for comfort. Luke did not share the
same ambition that I did, but he did have goals. Who knows?
Who knows if it was Luke whom God had sent to me to walk
down this path? Perhaps we needed each other. I was not sure
why God had intended for us to cross paths, but I did know it
was not a mistake.

I needed someone who was patient and would listen to me.
Luke validated my beauty, intelligence, and talent. Why would
I want to push him out of my life? I knew what everyone else
thought of me. I knew that my family did not respect my dreams.
I knew my parents were too closed-minded to want to allow me
to flee their close-knit nest. I knew my sister and I had a constant life of competition, of what I do not know. I never blamed
Phoebe for other people comparing me to her. Although I based
some of my actions on her acceptance, I never wanted to be
like her. I knew that my friends' lives were perhaps already con-
demned to their lost hopes and were waiting for me to join them.
At least with Luke I was on a pedestal, because I would eventually have a different destiny than most around us. The more
Luke believed in me, the more he was winning me over emotionally. Even though we resumed our friendship, I still kept my
distance physically. As the summer was coming to an end, Luke
and I had nothing more than a friendship that was maintained
with phone conversations. It was nice to know that when I felt
like the world was against me—there was always that one person
in my corner. At least Luke was thinking about me when I felt
like no one else was, and that was why I wanted him in my life.

One night a few weeks before I went to my new school, I
had a very spiritual moment. I had a dream about my brother
Angel. He was wearing a white tank top. He was using a small
Elmer's glue bottle and popsicle sticks, as I was using in real life
earlier that day that had once belonged to him. In the dream he

was upset that my sister and I had been using his belongings. I was trying to explain to him what we were doing, and how his absence made me feel.

"We were making crafty projects with your things. I miss you, because I feel alone sometimes without you. Phoebe and Joseph are always together, and I do not have anyone anymore," I said in the dream.

"I know you miss me," he told me. "I'm sorry."

I reached to hug him and said, "I wish you weren't gone," and began to cry.

Gasping for air, I awoke to a breathless feeling and was struggling to get it back as tears swept down my cheeks. It was a spiritually miraculous feeling. I missed my older brother and thought how sometimes life was unfair. Maybe without having realized it before, I had lost another partner in my life that made me want to avoid intimacy. Sometimes people leave, not by any choice of their own, and yet we seem to blame ourselves. Angel was always my golden angel watching over me. I had learned the hard way that life was too short not to always truly appreciate everyone in my life. No one ever knows when God's plan is to bring him to heaven.

A few days before I left for school in August, Luke called me. We had not talked for several weeks. He told me he missed me and wondered why I had not called in such a long time. "I looked you up in the phone book and called information because I misplaced your number," Luke told me. "Do you know you are unlisted? I really did. I know you don't believe me. Don't ever do that to me again, go so long without calling."

"I believe you," I responded. I believed that he did lose my number. "I did want to call you, but for some reason I just didn't; besides, I have been getting ready to start at a new school."

"Don't feel like you can't call me. You can call me whenever you want, anytime. If I'm not home, so what! Try again later.

You better make sure you keep in touch while you're gone," Luke said. I promised that I would stay in touch, and he was more at ease. I had reassured him that nothing would change. I was only moving less than an hour away.

The Saturday before I left for school, I went to a youth retreat. I wanted to show God that I was serious about walking down my path with Him and that I would not allow anyone to come between us. There was one man sharing his testimony, and he was telling us, "How dare the youth show up to the house of God, some people dressed like gangbangers, some with tattoos, boys with earrings and many with unusual piercings!" I felt bad for him, for who was he to judge us? He did not understand the community from which we were coming, the community of lost hopes; at least we had the courage to step foot in God's house, because we were seeking Him, because He had perhaps sent for us. Who knows, maybe those boys *were* gangbangers who needed God to remove them from their world. We all needed God to remove us from any negative surroundings so that we can follow His plan and not fall into the other temptations that many of our counterparts had already. That was why we were there, not to be judged by what we did in the past, but to help inspire a change for the betterment of our futures. We were there by choice to choose to change our mistakes, not to be reminded of them. God loves us all, does He not? God accepts us all, does He not? Before I went to bed that night, I prayed to God to keep me strong in this next journey, help me find all of which He wishes me to seek, to be with me, protect me, and watch over me. I prayed for the other youth and all those that judge God's lost sheep. I prayed for God to keep me emotionally strong as I vulnerably ventured into this new world where He had guided me. I prayed for the courage to battle those that tried to thrust me off my path.

God's Gift

"That's what makes you beautiful,"
but it's a painful quality.
"It's who you are,"
so it hurts to be me?

"Don't lose your sensitivity!"
But it's being taken away
by all the verbal punches,
the mean things that they say.

They may want to see me defeated;
perhaps they want to see me silent.
They become vicious.
They become violent.

They lunge their fists deep down in my heart,
rip out all my dreams and deliberately tear them apart.
Face to face, God keeps me strong.
He holds my head high and I pretend nothing's wrong.

Then alone at the altar
my head drops to the floor
and my tears shower out.
I cannot hold either anymore.

I blame my sensitivity; it let me down again.
God, when will it be my savior and not just a dead end?
My sensitivity is my weakness and sometimes my pain.
My sensitivity is the cause of my sadness again and again.

But without it, God, who would I be?
I wouldn't be beautiful; I wouldn't be me.

YZABELLE JIMÉNEZ MARTÍNEZ

The day I left for school, my brother Joseph, delivered me to the next destination of God's plan. I did not know what to expect. I felt sad that first night, away from my family. Several thoughts entered my mind. Would this new environment really be a better change for me? What would the people be like? Where would I find God? How will I avoid temptation? After the first night, the time quickly passed. And all my curiosities were soon discovered.

NEW CHRISTIANS OF ST. AMBROSE

...The body, however, is not for immorality, but for the Lord, and the Lord is for the body;...Do you not know that your body is a temple of the Holy Spirit within you, whom you have from God, and that you are not your own?...Therefore, whoever thinks he is standing secure should take care not to fall...There are different kinds of spiritual gifts but the same Spirit. There are different forms of service, but the same Lord:...To each individual the manifestation of the spirit is given for some benefit... Love never fails.

1 Corinthians 6:13,19, 10:12, 12:4-5,7, 13:8

I could not believe where I was. Not in Piano City! In a university getting closer to the goals that most people did not think I could reach. As soon as the first day passed, the first week did so too, and soon I got used to my new environment. It did take me a while to warm up to people and feel confident in fulfilling the goals that I had set for myself when I was first accepted. I focused on school and God and less on anything that would get between us. I had a professor that was impressed with my writing skills and asked if I would consider working in the writing lab as a tutor. She told me that she would write me a recommendation. She knew that they did not hire first semester students, but that it would be a mistake not to hire me now. Mrs. Kyria, the professor that recommended me, was the first person that I considered as an instrument of God while on this journey. I had allowed myself to trust her and let her help me. I would respect and adore her throughout my time at the university, for she was the first person that believed in me. The opportunity for which she advocated for me would open up other doors and windows of opportunities to move me forward on campus.

My success in school continued to give me a different kind of confidence than the confidence I perhaps tried to seek at one point in my life. I was moving forward with God. Although I wanted a career in journalism, I majored in English. I began to think about teaching as a way of giving back to the communities of lost hopes, and maybe God was pushing me in that direction. Based on statistics of my race, I was sure that Piano City was not the only city of lost hopes. I minored in journalism and Spanish. Working in the writing lab allowed me to share my gift. I was also exposed to so many different topics about life. I read a number of student essays. I benefited from their research. I saw many people learn to become stronger and more confident writers, and it gave me pleasure to see people feel good about themselves.

Gelline was a tutor I met while working in the writing lab. She was an editor for the school newspaper and in many of my English classes. She told me that they had openings on the newspaper and to go meet the editor-in-chief. Writing for the newspaper continued to boost my confidence and I felt that it was God giving me these opportunities, allowing me to learn the skills that one day would benefit me in meeting His plan. I dedicated myself to being an editor, to being a writing tutor, and, of course, to being a full-time student. Lastly, I involved myself in the college's Latino organization, *Poder*. Being a part of this organization allowed me to continue to make social changes for the Latino community of Saint Ambrose, Chicago, and this country. It was through this part of my journey where I met a very special friend, Solomon. Solomon was a sophomore; he was almost three years younger than I was, but wise in experiences of life. Once I got comfortable in my new environment and gathered the confidence to create new relationships with people, it would be Solomon I would let inside.

Within a few weeks of school, I heard from Luke. I had not seen him in about six months, with the exception of our Fourth of July run-in, and we had not talked in a month. He had expressed his concern about me not having called him in so long. "I have a new focus," I told him, "that's all."

"You promised you would keep in touch," Luke reminded me.

"I know. I'm sorry, but this is just much more challenging than I expected." I knew Luke thought I was talking about school, but part of me was also referring to our relationship.

"Why?" Luke asked.

"Why? Because this is my future, that's why! I am just really involved and just really busy," I responded.

"I know, but I miss you and miss talking to you," he said.

"Well, I'm sorry, I just have different priorities than before."

"School?" he said.

"Well, yes, school. And along with my classes I have a full plate of tutoring and working on the paper and being involved in an organization," I said.

"I'm proud of you," he said.

"What?" I responded surprisingly.

"I'm proud of you. You're doing what you said you would be doing when we first met. That's why I miss you so much. You're such a good person and you make me want to be a better person," he said with sincerity.

I do not know where his thoughts were coming from, but I did not feel the same. On the contrary, I thought, then why was he trying to hold me back? Luke was a temptation. I cared for him so much, but what kind of a relationship would we have? Where would it lead us? It was around this time last year that we met, and I felt as though he provoked so much within me in such a short period of time. I had that kind of connection with people, though, to make them feel comfortable around me, especially men. Deep down inside, I questioned how good of a person I was. Sometimes I felt like a hypocrite throughout my journey with God, as if some of my actions offended Him. The guilt and shame would eat away at my soul, especially when people praised me on how I lived my life. I sometimes felt like these compliments were just as hindering as negative judgments and criticisms.

"I just get really busy, and by the time I might get a chance to call you I feel like it might be too late, or too early," I said.

"You can write me," Luke suggested.

"What?" I asked.

"You can write me a letter, if that is easier for you. I can give you my address and you can write me letters," he said.

He knew that writing for me was a lot more conducive to my schedule and my interests. He knew that it was so much easier for me to express myself in writing than to do it verbally. There was too much fear in words for me when it came to conversation, but I always had the perfect words when it came to writing them down. It was that instant response or reaction that I was not always ready for; it takes time for my emotions to process. Other times, my hypersensitivity takes over and I cannot control my initial emotions. I learned a while back that when you share your feelings, people that you love will not always support you. At times I felt as though I tried so hard to accomplish what was important to me, and what I wanted was never good enough for others. When I kept my feelings to myself, I did not get heard, but sometimes when I shared my feelings, they still seemed to get ignored. So either way, people would not always support my emotional demands. Mrs. Kyria taught me that people will always judge you, and even the people that you love will let you down emotionally, but there is always at least one person that will help you cope, one person in whom you can confide and trust, one that will listen to you and help you any way they can. Depending on the situation, it may not always necessarily be the same person. Sometimes it may not even be someone that you know well, but that is how a God-given friendship gets started.

"When am I going to see you again?" He had asked me this with such eager anticipation.

"I don't know; maybe next weekend we can get together," I said.

I was afraid to see Luke, though. Here was a man, whom I could love or with whom I was already in love. He would push me to be in his life but was not prepared to give me what I wanted. Sometimes I felt as though it was God trying to protect my heart, knowing that he was not the one, but was I refusing to listen? I continued to hold on to Luke. He made me feel like I had a purpose, which was the role he was taking away from God.

I wrote Luke a letter inviting him to come down to my campus, which I knew he would never do, although he acted as if it was quite an honor. He used his son and his job as an excuse. He called me shortly after that to tell me how much he missed me, but it was hard to continue believing his words when his actions were more apparent. His words seemed so strong and sincere, but how come they were never enough to motivate some action that would have been more convincing? Despite his actions, I was not ready to lose hope in him.

I had not gone home for a few weeks, even though I told Luke that I would and eventually I missed my family. I decided to go home for a weekend, and that was when Luke called and asked to see me. It had been several months since the last time I saw him, again with exception of the display at the Taste of Chicago. He asked me to go out to a bar with him and his friends. I told him I forgot my ID at school. "Do you just want to come over and watch a movie?" he asked.

"Of course, I'd love to," I said. I knew that I was the one dismissing him all the other times he tried to see me. I asked myself, Leizel, why are you so afraid? I probably knew the answer to that, but in theory life is always easier than actually going through the motions. He picked me up. I felt nervous. I could not believe that I had not seen him in so long. We did have an amazing night though, a night that would lead us into the morning.

Luke no longer lived out of the basement of his parent's home. Although his son still had his own room, Luke now had an entertainment room upstairs, next door to his son's room. It had a comfy couch, a bookshelf with a few books, CDs, movies, and a television. And in a separate room, he had his bed. He walked me over to his couch. He led me by the hand, and I followed behind. I sat down, not quite sure how to act. Should I control my emotions? Do I conceal my excitement, my nervousness?

"What do you want to watch? We never finished watching, *Braveheart*, did we?" Luke asked as he sat down next to me.

"No, but I don't think I want to attempt it again," I responded with a stiff smile.

"What's wrong?" He asked sensing a difference in me. I had my hands to myself, rested on my lap.

"What do you mean?" I was also afraid to make eye contact with him.

"You seem uptight. You seem different, like you changed, a lot." He said as he grabbed my hand, indicating that it was okay to take it off my lap and place it any where else I wanted.

My nervousness was making me feel shy and a little insecure, qualities he had never seen in me. Part of Luke's attraction to me was that I was always confident. I do not think he liked this shy, insecure person that he was meeting for the first time. I was not sure why I was feeling so much apprehension, maybe because of what I felt, or wondering if he still felt the same about me.

We awkwardly watched a very long movie, and sat side by side making comments about the scenes we liked. We did not touch. I understood why he thought I was different. We used to have such a comfortable level of interaction, intimacy, and chemistry. Here I was holding back, and he did not know what to make of it. I felt as though he did not want to do anything that might make me uncomfortable. I had to be the one to give him the indication that I still had feelings for him, that I was still attracted to him, that I still desired him, and that I too missed him as much as he expressed that he missed me. Tired, I rested my head on his shoulder. It was all Luke needed to respond to me and know that we were both going to fall into the same trap. He placed his arm around me. When the movie ended he asked me if I wanted to go home or hang out a little longer. I felt unfulfilled. There was so much that I needed to know. I needed to know how he felt about me. What did he want or expect from me? When were we going to see each other again? In another seven or eight months? At that moment I had to follow my heart instead of my head. I remained with Luke. I needed to see what would happen next, what was possible of happening next.

He arose from the couch and headed toward the entertainment center and shut off the television. I took the liberty of lying down and stretching across the entire couch. He came back over, and before I knew it, we had managed a kiss, and then another. We had moved from the couch into his bedroom and onto his bed. We spent four hours talking. We reminisced of our merriment once shared in better times of past encounters.

He asked me about Judith and told me about how James was doing. He asked about school. What kind of articles was I writing? He told me that he was proud of me again. He wanted me to know that he was impressed that when we met I had a goal, and I had reached it.

One thing we did not discuss was our future. I did not know where this would lead. Although he was the one asking all the questions, I was much too afraid of what I would hear if I asked about our future. I was, however, proud of myself for not having fallen into the tarnishing exploitations that at times rip me away from my most beloved Father.

Back at school, I tried not to concentrate too much on what would become of me and Luke. I concentrated on school, doing homework, studying, tutoring, and keeping up with the news section of the newspaper. Solomon and I began to spend a lot of time together. We would study and have lunch together. He was a graphics art major. Solomon was tall; he had one length hair that came just over his shoulders, like Jesus. He was a *rockero*, into Spanish Rock. He even hosted his own Spanish rock radio program on the school's station with his friend, Eric. The media building was a facility that housed all the school's communication activities. It was located at the far end of campus. Solomon was mysterious, and polite and respectful of people. He tried hard to be an individual, both inside and out. The strongest characteristic about Solomon was that he was wise and philosophical. He liked to help people with their problems and offer them advice. He wanted people to recognize their self-worth. He was a great listener and he encouraged people to take risks that their hearts desired. He was supportive of what people wanted to try. He had asked me to help him with a paper one day and was surprisingly pleased at his grade when he got it back, and so he continued to come to me for help. He had a poetic style of writing that revealed a sensitive and considerate side of him.

I had begun to develop a crush on Solomon. I liked being around him; I loved his optimism. He was funny and fun. But the last thing I needed in my life was another guy rejecting me or controlling my emotions. So I kept my feelings to myself. I also figured it was natural for me to develop feelings for someone that I saw almost on a daily basis. Based on the last encounter with Luke, a relationship that was not ideal and challenging my self-worth as a woman, having a crush on someone like Solomon made my life more idealistic. It made it easier to deal with Luke.

A week had gone by and I still had not heard from Luke. I focused my energy and passion on my studies as usual. One day alone in my room, trying to focus on the words in front of me in my literature anthology, I was reading this story about love and second chances; even though one marriage did not work out, the next one more than made up for it. Was love something that would ever happen for me? Honestly, I did not see it. Maybe being in love was not in my near future because it was just a distraction from my own professional goals and the plans God had for me. I decided that after my B.A. I would go to graduate school. I did not need to be in love to be the person I wanted to be. It was also then that I made a pact with myself that I would not be in a committed relationship until I had accomplished all my goals, because all relationships did were distract me from my goals and God's plan.

Saturday night I had received a call from Luke. "What are you doing? I wanted to see if you were in town this weekend. I was wondering if you wanted to come over and watch the sunrise with me," Luke said.

"Yes." I said, "I am here this weekend. I did not expect to hear from you."

"I would have called you earlier, but I just woke up and started eating my dinner. I wasn't sure if you wanted to talk to me anymore since you hadn't called me. I have no idea how girls think. So I thought I'd just take a chance," he informed me.

"Yeah, it's cool, we can hang out," I told him.

I found his comment about not knowing how women thought was amusing, because the irony of it was that I also did not know how men thought. I was happy that he wanted to see me, because I thought it would be a long time before I heard from him again. From our last encounter I had felt so strongly about how much I wanted to be with him. This time I was not as strong, but the rapture of our connection together was emotionally and physically satisfying. I remembered again how relaxed and safe I felt in his arms. This was the feeling that I feared and what made me so uptight the last time we were together. It seemed so quick how this one person could break the reigns of God's grip.

The next few days I could not get what Luke and I did out of my mind. I began to wonder how he felt about me. What he wanted from me. What he expected from me. And there it was, the negative effect of temptation. This was not what should be going through my mind. For the next few days I went through the motions of school like a robot in order to make it to the weekend to see if Luke would call me, to know if he wanted to see me again. I tried to talk myself into understanding that school was my priority; Luke and anything else were all minor roles in my life that could not interfere with my purpose. The whole week, all I did was look forward to the next weekend, wondering, "Will he or won't he?" And when the weekend rolled around, it was me who called Luke this time, only, he did not answer, and Friday, Saturday, and Sunday came and went, and I did not hear from him. There it was, the reason why I hated falling in love, or should I say, falling into temptation.

So I returned to school Sunday night with my "why me" disappointed disposition. I went through my normal "returning from the weekend" routine. I unloaded my laundry and popped in about three or four rooms to see how my friends enjoyed their weekends. They were usually all in one room until we all got back from home. Once we said our good nights, I went back to my dorm and mentally obsessed over Luke.

I had class Monday morning at eight. I did not act like anything was bothering me, though. I went on with my day as if nothing was eating up my insides. I went to the writing lab for two hours after class to tutor. I had lunch with Solomon. I had my Shakespearean literature course in the afternoon, then Philosophy 101, and after that, the newspaper. With exception of my journalism courses and a few English courses, I was not that engaged in terms of what I was learning and how irrelevant I found it all to be in my life at the time. I do not know why I felt like this. I do not know what I expected my future to be like, and I did not want to think about the future that much, but I could not help it. On one hand I had so many future dreams, ideas, and goals, and on the other hand I wondered what would become of my future.

During the week Luke had called. Since I did not answer he left me a message asking me to call him back. I did not call him back right away, because I was on the phone. When I did finally get around to calling him back, he was no longer home. In the back of my mind I prayed for the guts to ask Luke why he had not called. Why he did not want to see me last weekend. Was he with someone else? How did he feel about me? That was why I was scared. I wanted him to know how his actions disappointed me and I wanted to know what he expected from me. But I was always so afraid of the truth, I wondered if I would even have the courage to confront him about how I felt. You know that phrase, "You can't handle the truth?" Well that was me. I literally cannot handle the truth. My emotions are like fragile crystal. They are thin and delicate. His words had the power to shatter my emotional soul.

I called Luke a couple of times after the first phone call I made, but both times he was on his way out. He said, "I called you the other day, how come you didn't call me back?"

"I did, you just weren't there," I responded.

"Oh, no one told me," he said, "but I will give you a call back when I have a chance." Again I felt rejected. His comments, however, restrained me from calling him again. He eventually called me a few days later. I could not help but behave in a spiteful way with him, which was a behavior I had never portrayed before. Was it a good thing that for the first time I gathered the courage to lash out at him? I hated acting like this, though. It seemed over dramatic.

"What are you doing?" He began the conversation.

"Studying, what do you think I am doing?" I responded defensively.

"I don't know, that's why I asked," Luke said.

"The first week of November is mid-terms week," I said.

"Oh, well did you want me to call you later?" he asked.

"If you don't want to talk to me now, then do whatever you want," I replied.

"Why are you acting like this?" he asked.

"Because I don't even know why you are calling me. When I call you, you are always busy or blowing me off," I said resentfully.

"I don't mean to make you feel like I am blowing you off. I call you because I like you. I like to talk to you. I don't want you to think that I only want to talk to you or see you when you're out here. I want you to know that I think about you. I don't mean to make you feel like I am blowing you off, but it was just coincidence that when you called me I was on my way out the door," he said.

There was so much that I wanted to say and ask him, but it was never in my nature. I could never stand up for myself, for my feelings. I do not know of what I was so afraid; why could I not do it? His response made me feel a little more at ease. Maybe I was just over reacting. "Oh, I guess," I responded, "well sometimes I just get upset."

"I'm sorry if I upset you. I can call you back if you want, later tonight, or another day if you're going to be busy," he said.

"Okay, I'll just talk to you later, then," I said.

A few days later Luke called me again, and I figured he would, because he was probably intrigued by the change in my behavior. I am sure he was curious to see if I was feeling better. I finally told him that something had been bothering me. I asked him if I was the only woman with whom he was involved. He said, "To be honest, yeah. I am just not in a great place right now in my life. I like you; I like spending time with you, but you know I can't give you more than that. But on the same note, I am not bringing anyone else into the picture."

"Oh, I see," I responded. I was not completely satisfied with what he said, but he probably thought that I should have been.

I tried talking myself into having the strength and courage to confront the situation. One activity that helped me was praying a rosary. Most rosaries are comforting, especially when they are made of beautiful fragile stones or crystals. I feel as though I am holding the delicacies of pain, anger, or fear physically in my hands and literally offering them to God, Jesus, the Holy Spirit, and the Virgin Mary, telling them that I no longer want these destructive infestations hording my sense of faith, hope and spirituality. Other times I pray for the continual blessings of love, happiness, and success for which I am grateful. The most symbolic rosary is the one where the beads resemble actual roses. A rose is an obvious choice, for it symbolizes love, which is the greatest gift from God. So why does love make my life so difficult? I always felt like praying for love was so superficial, but maybe if I actually prayed for it more often, my love life would be different. Although a purpose for praying the rosary today is to pray for the souls of the deceased; the rosary was a form of fighting the heresy that denied that Jesus was a real human being on earth; therefore the act of praying it encompasses the faith in the life and emotions of Jesus here on earth, living among His brothers and sisters. It has taught us to get to know God and to believe in the three stages of Jesus's life, the mysteries of His glory, joy, and pain. We as humans experience these same emotions and can feel cleansed spiritually, and become filled with more courage, ambition, and perseverance to take on the world, or at least our little corner of it. It is at these times I am not always good or strong or courageous. Sometimes I am weak and scared and ashamed. With all the challenges of Luke and school, my safest haven of comfort and security is with God. He gives me the strength to fight my spiritual battles.

In My Father's Arms

In my Father's arms
is where I run for strength,
in my world where there is temptation,
there is deception and there is pain,
people who use me, and judge me;
it's where I go when I feel fear and I feel shame.

In the warmth of my Father's arms
I can forget the cold, soulless eyes
that do not understand my defeated cries;
but His protective arms do,
extending to support my fall,
when I am in the center of a whirlwind.

In my loving Father's arms
I am forgiven of all my sins;

I am perfection; I have no flaws.
I am naturally beautiful and full of grace!
I am given the purity and courage of a dove,
with soaring wings—mended and strong.
I fight the enemy, with patience and love,
and the evil for those who cannot see
because they are spiritually weak.

Because of His strength,
because of His love,
because of His forgiveness,
because of my loving Father's arms.

For the next few weeks, I concentrated on school and spent time admiring Solomon. I liked to hear him speak. Luke and I were going through another wave of distance. Judith got married at the end of November, during a Thanksgiving weekend. She was expecting. I felt disappointed that I had lost her, but, of course, as her best friend, I was happy for her. Her marriage would later have quite an impact on my life, more than I could have ever imagined. I spent that night dancing with my family and friends, honoring her blessed day. I watched another of my friend's dreams and hopes begin to change. I myself had hoped that God would help me change my heart so that I could let go of Luke and welcome in someone new. When I had gone out for some air a boy came over to me, and I knew it was the start of a new chapter in my life.

THE SUFFERINGS ACCORDING TO JOB

…Your sons and daughters were eating and drinking wine in the house of their eldest brother, when suddenly a great wind came across the desert and smote the four corners of the house. It fell upon the young people and they are dead…the Lord restored the prosperity of Job, after he had prayed for his friends; the Lord even gave to Job twice as much as he had before.

Job 1:18-19, 42:10

The boy who had come to speak with me looked younger than me but it turned out he was only a little more than a year younger than I was.

"What's your name?" he said.

"Leizel," I replied.

"Do you know the bride or the groom?" he asked.

"Both actually, but mainly the bride, and you?" I asked him.

"I work with the bride's husband, what do you do?" he inquired.

"I go to school in Chicago," I said.

"Yeah, what school?" he asked.

"Saint Ambrose University," I answered.

"What is that, a college, you're in college? How old are you?" He continued to interrogate me.

"Twenty-two. How old are you?" I asked.

"Twenty, but twenty-one next month." He said as-a-matter-of-factly, wanting to convince me of something. "So what do you do at school?"

"Learn. Read. Write," I responded.

"What?" he asked confused.

"I'm an English major and a journalist," I said.

"So where do you live?" he asked curiously.

"I live on campus at school," I said. "What about you?" I asked.

"I live here, in Verde Altos, with my aunt and uncle," he informed me.

Eventually I learned that his name was Job. He had been working for three years at the paint company where Judith's husband worked. I was not that attracted to him, but he seemed kind and considerate and impressed that I was in college. Perhaps it was because most girls my age in our dead-end town were mothers by now and looking for someone to not only care for them, but also their babies. Job and I exchanged numbers. I was able to use him as a distraction from Luke. He seemed pretty average to me, the same hair, style of dress, just the same look as most guys from the small "urbanized" suburbs. We spoke a few times on the phone, and eventually he asked me out on a date, and I agreed.

Our first date was his company's Christmas party. He picked me up in his blue Cadillac, a car of which he was very proud, and also from which he had received quite a bit of confidence. I came out of the house and he opened the car door for me. "You look nice," Job said.

"I'm sorry, but I did not get a chance to finish getting ready. I had to move out of my dorm today," I said.

I was not even sure what I was supposed to wear. The party was at the Star Plaza Hotel. I felt like I would be a princess at a ball, and that was what I was supposed to look like, had I had enough time to make myself into a princess. At that moment when I stepped into his blue chariot, he looked at my hands and he went ballistic.

"What's up with your nails?" Job asked.

"I told you that I did not have enough time to finish getting ready. I wasn't able to do them," I said.

"But they're all chipped. It looks tacky," he responded.

"Well, I'm sorry, I didn't know how important manicures were to you. What? Are we having tea with the Queen at Buckingham Palace and all!" I said sarcastically.

"I know you are a busy college girl, but this night is important to me, and I want everything to be perfect. You understand, don't you? Where can we stop to get some nail polish remover?" he asked.

I was not sure what to think about Job. He was so rough around the edges. He was so open and honest in an uneducated, blunt sort of way. I was not sure if I was going to be able to get close to him, but I certainly tried to give him a chance. I had decided to move forward from my relationship with Luke and try to let go of him and let someone else sweep me off my feet. I just was not too sure if Job was the guy for the job.

The night of my first date with Job, I clearly felt humbled. Here was this guy that had taken me to this important event in his life, feeling proud of who I was only after two weeks of knowing me, and all I could do was feel sorry for myself and think about a guy that probably had too many of his own issues to think of me in that way.

Because the party was at a hotel, many of Job's friends rented a suite, and afterwards he had taken me to meet them. First of all, Deacon, a friend of Luke's was there; seeing him made me think of Luke and made me feel closer to him. It also gave me a sense of confidence, because I thought in my mind how our friend would tell Luke that I was at his party on a date with another guy. That thought led to believing that this would make him jealous, and maybe want me more. Maybe Luke did not even care. I had so much to learn back then. Deacon had also mentioned that perhaps Luke and James might stop by later. That in itself was reason alone to want to stay. Although I had wanted to stay, it appeared that Job did not. He wanted to spend quiet quality time with me, getting to know me. Subconsciously, I knew that I probably feared that. I had begun to mingle and have a good time with the people there. Job kept asking me if we could leave, and I rudely ignored him. Before I knew it, he discreetly turned around and walked out of the room. I was too into my own agenda to notice or even care. I wanted to ignore the encounter with my feelings, the sadness that I had for longing to be there with Luke instead of Job, the sadness I had of knowing that I felt rejected by Luke. I even wanted to avoid allowing Job to get to know me better; therefore, I rejected him. I did not want to let him in my soul, to find out who I was. Several minutes had gone by, and I had not even thought of going after Job. Deacon, although not the most considerate person I had known, was intuitive enough to know what the right thing was for me to do.

"Don't be stupid," Deacon said.

"What do you mean? Why are you talking to me like that?" I asked.

"Because that's how you're acting. What are you waiting around here for? Luke? Meanwhile there is a nice guy that you came with. It's pretty messed up, what you're doing. You're supposed to be the nice girl. That's probably why he brought you here in the first place. You don't just bring any kind of girl to these things. You bring your wife, or someone that deserves it.

You need to go and find Job. You came here with him. He is the one you should be worrying about." Deacon had shed some light on the situation.

I just stood there looking at him, thinking to myself, what is wrong with me? And then I responded, "You're right."

I turned around and walked out the door. I looked down the hallway to my left and then to my right, hoping to see Job. I felt bad for him. He was the unlucky guy that caught me on the rebound. We were on the third floor, right above the pool area. I looked down over the handrail, and there was Job, sitting on a lounge chair, pathetically alone, in an unlit area beside the pool. The only lights on were the pool lights that shimmered underneath the water. I saw the reflection of a girl I did not recognize, someone I never wanted to be. There it was, a face without a shine. I could see how men might have been attracted to it, but at that moment, I did not like what I saw behind that reflection. I could only imagine how God was probably looking down on me.

I found my way to Job and slowly and subtly stepped into his presence and asked, "Can I sit with you?"

"Are you sure you want to? Maybe you'd rather be up there with those guys," Job said.

"No. I came here with you, and I want to be with you right now," I said softly.

"Are you sure?" he asked.

"Yes, if you'll let me. I'm sorry I acted like such a jerk." I said apologetically.

He looked up at me with misty eyes, and I felt like an even bigger jerk.

"Are you okay?" I asked.

"Yeah, I just felt sad," he replied.

"I'm really sorry." I said.

"No, it wasn't you," said Job.

"Well, then what's wrong?" I asked him.

"You know how I told you that I live with my uncle, and my aunt?"

"Yes," I said.

"I was just thinking about my parents." I remained quiet and just let him talk. "I miss them. They were killed in a car accident. Sometimes I think of them as my guardian angels. They should be watching over me. I pray to them and tell them what is important to me and how I wanted this night to go."

"It's not your parent's fault that I am such a jerk. The night isn't over. We had a nice time so far, before the hotel suite, didn't we?" I said.

"Yeah, I guess so," he said.

I sat with Job on the lounge chair, and we spent about two hours sitting at the poolside, talking, getting to know each other better. He was telling me about how he wanted to be a mortician and own his own mortuary. I thought, morbid, but maybe it was because of the fact that he experienced the loss of both his parents and knew what families needed during an emotionally challenging time. I encouraged him to go back to school and take business classes. I did not know much about that particular occupation, but I was always pushing Latinos into going to school. In addition to our conversation, we spent the early night watching the waterfall splash into the swimming pool. I could see my cascading face begin to change, but I knew it was going to take a lot more than one good decision to change my soul. What I did not know was whether I had the will in me to change, to give up on Luke and try to find that spark with Job.

Job and I got past the first big date. I was home for a month, and he and I went out about once a week. He worked at a paint factory Monday through Friday, and Saturdays were our date nights. By this time Luke was out of the picture for sure. Whether he would be a part of my life anymore, I did not know.

Job and I spent New Year's Eve together. Judith and her husband had their first gathering as a couple at their home, and I invited Job. He brought me a Christmas gift. Of course, he was one of those people with whom you agree no gifts and he does it anyway.

"It's nothing big. I just thought of you when I saw it," Job said as he handed me a box with several objects inside.

I opened his gifts with a small lack of desire only because I felt guilty. "It's cute." It was a female stuffed monkey.

"Here, press this button." It whistled the sexy call whistle.

"It's cute," I responded with a fake grin.

"I got her for Monkey so he wouldn't be lonely when you're out with me," he said.

I smiled. Monkey was a stuffed animal I talked about a lot that my mother bought me when I was sixteen because I was getting my tonsils removed. "Thank you."

"Look there's something else," he said pointing.

There was a jewelry box and I prayed it was not jewelry. I opened it. "Tickets?"

"Yeah," he said eagerly.

"A Bull's game? You didn't have to do that," I said.

"But I did. They're for about two weeks from now. I hope you don't mind taking me?" he said.

"Well, why did you make me agree that we weren't gonna get gifts and then you go and get a gift? That doesn't feel fair. It makes me look like I'm not grateful," I said.

"You don't have to think of it as a Christmas gift," responded Job.

"Well, why else would you give me a gift?" I asked, not sure if I wanted to hear the answer.

"To say thank you, because I'm grateful," he said.

"For what?" I cringed at the thought of what he would tell me. I prayed that he did not tell me something gushy that would make me feel guiltier.

"Because of your advice, I decided to go back to school. I was going for a couple of semesters part time and didn't really feel like going anymore. But you make me want to be a better person," he said.

And there it was; the same nonsense that Luke gave me. I know I should be flattered, but it made me feel like a hypocrite again. My intentions were never to make anyone feel like they are not good enough for me or "as good as me," because I am human too and I am not perfect. Going to college is not what makes me a good person. Loving and following God is what makes me a good person; and I am not always good at that. I could stand to be a better person too. What are they measuring themselves to when it comes to me?

I did feel guilty for taking Job's gifts. Mainly because I did not know how I felt about him. Even though he was a nice guy, there was something missing that I longed for in a man. There was something missing that was preventing me from falling for this guy, or perhaps wanting to fall for this guy. I knew part of it was because I still missed Luke. I did the only thing I could do, and that was to pray about it, and ask God why he brought Job into my life. Ask God to help me know what His plan was for me and if I am on the right path.

One Friday night when I was out with friends, I saw Luke at a local club. His son's mother was there too. Luke just followed her around looking angry. I did not know if he was angry because she was not at home with their son, or because she did not want to be with him. Of course Luke and I exchanged greetings, but it was obvious we were both distracted from the typical reaction we would get from just the mere sight of each other. I know by what he was preoccupied. I was racked with guilt for even running into him. I felt as though I was wrong for feeling something, but I tried to fight it or hide it out of respect for Job. Job was not even with me that night, and I still felt a small obligation to him. That weekend I wrote Luke a letter letting him know that I thought it would be best if we no longer talked anymore. I think I did it because it hurt me more to see him so attached to his past, trying so hard to regain it, that he wanted nothing more for his future. So what was I? I did not mail the letter right away. I waited until I was back at school.

Job would call me about twice a week so he would not feel like he was disturbing my studies. I never had to call Job. He was so reliable and predictable. The week I was back at school, Job called me Thursday evening. "Hello," I answered.

"Hey, you busy?" Job asked.

"Always, but I can talk for a little bit," I responded.

"How was your first week back?" he asked.

"Good, busy. How are your classes?" I inquired.

"They're okay. I guess some of the teachers are a little boring. I have to study a lot," he said.

"That's normal." I had to study a lot, too, I guess, it was more of just getting the work done and reading than studying, but I wanted to sound supportive.

"I liked having you home. I miss you. I think about you a lot," he said.

"I'll be home in a few days."

"I'm done for the night. Don't stay up too late. Have a good night. I'll call you later," he said.

That weekend I went home, Job and I went out on Friday night and we had our first fight. We had just finished watching *Titanic*; we were sitting in the theatre after the movie, and he was teary-eyed.

"What's wrong?" I asked Job.

"What do you mean what's wrong? The movie was sad," he replied.

"Oh, I didn't really like it," I said.

"Why?" he asked.

"Because it was unrealistic," I responded.

"*No*, you didn't like it because you have no heart!" We started to walk back to the car in silence. And he noticed I was not talking. "Do you want to get dinner?" he asked.

"No, I just want to go home now." I said, rather upset.

"Why, what's wrong?" he asked.

"You insulted me, just because I didn't like the movie. What? Did you write it? Did you make a cameo appearance and I didn't notice? Because we don't agree on something, you're going to insult me?" I replied.

"You made fun of me because I was crying," he argued.

"No, I didn't make fun of you. I asked you what was wrong, and I just said that I didn't like the movie. You got upset by that. Just take me home. I just want to go home," I said.

"Fine, if that's what you want."

"That's what I want," I said.

When I got home, I sat on my bed in the dark. It was quiet, since there was no one home. On one hand, Job had a point. I hated expressing my emotions. On the other hand, he was wrong. I did have a heart, only it was well protected. It learned love did not last forever, so why bother letting it exist at all. My heart was hurt and scared. I could not help myself; out of spite, I called Luke, but no one answered. At least with Luke there were no expectations. He was honest about being emotionally unavailable. I was the one that was not being honest about how I was not emotionally available. Maybe that is why it was easier with Luke. Maybe I liked the fact that he was not emotionally available. A few minutes later the phone rang; I got up to see who it was. I did not want to talk to Job at that moment. I just needed some time to think about what I wanted, but on the caller ID it happened to be who I wanted.

"Hello," I answered the phone.

"Hey, what are you doing?" said the voice on the other end.

"Nothing, what's up?" I asked.

"I was in the bathroom when you called," responded Luke.

"Oh," I said.

"I got your letter. I didn't understand why you wrote me a good-bye letter. Where did it come from that all of a sudden you don't want to be friends with me? I thought I was never going to see or talk to you again. Then I see that you called, and I don't know what to think. The last time I saw you was at the club, and you barely gave me five minutes of your time. You seemed all busy with other guys," said Luke.

"I don't know why I wrote that." I did not know what to say to him. I wanted to tell him that he was the one that was "all busy" with his son's mother, but I did not want to talk about her. It was her fault that he was not emotionally available and would not move forward. However, I realized that we had that in common.

"Did I do something?" Luke inquired.

"It's just hard sometimes to try and be your friend when I want more, but then I also feel like I don't want to not be friends with you. I guess on some level I do like sharing parts of my life with you," I replied.

Luke and I fell asleep talking on the phone, and the next morning Job called me. I knew I had intentions to call him and had been deciding what to say to him, but of course it was probably on his mind all night, and so he could not wait until the morning to repair all the damages. So I answered the phone ready to take on the responsibility. "Hello."

"Leizel?" said Job.

"Yes," I replied.

"How are you? What are you doing?" Job said nervously.

"Just woke up," I said.

"I hope I didn't wake you," he said.

"No."

"I wanted to say I was sorry about yesterday. I overreacted," said Job.

"No, you didn't. You were right to get frustrated with me. I know you're confused about how I feel about you. I like you, Job, but I have a lot going on in my life. If you have the patience for me and you want to keep dating that's fine, but if you don't want to, and feel like you're wasting your time, then I understand," I explained to him.

"I'm not wasting my time. I like you, and I can give you the patience you need," he said.

"Oh. So everything is okay; we're cool?" I asked.

"Yeah, but I'm still really sorry for talking to you that way," he said.

My relationship with Job continued to progress, and it became a routine. I was at school all week and only saw him on the weekends and talked a few times a week after he had finished his homework. I could tell school was taking a toll on him and it seemed like it was something that he did not want to do anymore. Regardless of how patient Job said he was going to be, I could tell he was getting impatient as to how slow our relationship was moving.

One time during a phone conversation, he caught me off guard. "So, what's up with me and you?" Job asked.

"What do you mean?" I asked.

"When are you going to come around? I really like you. Sometimes I think I love you, but I hate you," he said.

"Oh, all right, well, I'm not really sure what that means, but we had this conversation. If you feel like I am just wasting your time, then you are more than welcome to move on without me," I explained.

"I don't want to," he said.

"I like you, Job, and I think you're a great guy, but just give me a little more time. Relationships are just not my priority right now. School is," I said.

"I get it," he replied, but I was not so sure that he did.

Job liked to take me wherever he knew we would run into his friends, especially to his friends' get-togethers. One Saturday night we had plans with another couple. Mark was his friend from his old neighborhood before he came to live with his uncle. They had plans to go to this party. Every time Job left my side to use the restroom, get food or a drink, or talk with his friends, this random girl would come over and talk to me. She would only do it when he left my side.

"So how long have you guys been going out?" asked the strange girl.

"Just a few of months," I responded.

"Where did you meet?" she asked.

"At a wedding," I replied.

"You guys look cute together. He seems like a really nice guy," she said.

"Thanks, yeah, he is a nice guy," I agreed.

"What does he do?" she asked.

"He works in a factory," I said.

"Where do you work?" she continued asking questions about us.

"I don't really. I go to school and work on campus," I said.

"Oh, what are you gonna be? What school do you go to?" she asked.

"Saint Ambrose, in Chicago, to be a journalist or teacher or something like that," I said impatiently.

Job came back, and the girl jumped up from the couch. She did not say anything to him. I wondered if they even knew each other. He sat down next to me on the couch. He was so comfortable around me. He would hold my hand and rest our hands on my knee. The guilt of not feeling the same way for him was eating at me, and frankly, I did not know how much longer I could go on with this feeling inside. "Are you having fun?" Job asked me.

"It's okay," I said.

"We can leave if you want," suggested Job. "Mark and his girl are gonna stay."

"It's your party. I'm fine." I could see that girl watching us. "Do you know that girl?" I said, pointing in her direction.

"That's Mark's cousin. Come on, we can leave. Let's go get something to eat," he said.

"Why does she keep looking at us? Does she like you?" I asked.

As we walked out, Job led me by the hand, and Mark's cousin said to me as I was walking out with Job, "Don't break his heart!"

I was scared to be in a relationship with Job. It was not just that I was afraid to get hurt, but I was well on my way to accomplishing my dreams and goals. Maybe one of the reasons Job liked me was not because I was in school, but because I was actually doing something with my life. The closer I got to reaching my goals, the more I feared that they would never come true. What would happen if we were to get together? Would he want to get married? Would we have a bunch of children? What about his goals? Would he always work in a factory? Would he ever finish school? Being in a relationship at this point would just be a huge transition for which I was not ready. Then it occurred to me, how exactly would God say that Job fits into my plan? And God had answered my prayer. God had put it all into perspective for me. It was not that I belonged with someone like Job, or that He did not want me with someone like Luke. What God wanted was for me to continue down His path. I was on the right track to meet God's greater plan. It was then that He let me know, that until I reached my educational goals, there was no need to be in a committed relationship with any man. I knew my relationship with Job had to end, I just did not know how or when. I did not want to break his heart. I also knew that Luke and I did not belong in a relationship, either, but how would I let him go without my heart breaking?

The weekend before Valentine's Day, I stayed at school. I had a lot of homework, and Job did not believe me.

"Don't break my heart," he would tell me, just like Mark's cousin.

"I just have a lot of work to do, and I am mostly going to be in my room all weekend," I said.

"And you're not going out?" he asked.

"I don't know; if something comes up with the girls then maybe, but mainly I just have a lot of homework," I said.

"Just don't break my heart," he repeated.

"Stop saying that. I won't, at least not today. Just kidding! I'll see you next weekend, Friday, on Valentine's Day. I promise," I assured him.

"All right. Have a good week-end. Call me if you get bored," he suggested.

"Bye," I replied.

After I hung up the phone, I picked up a brochure that I saw on campus. It was about a new study abroad program that the university was trying to expand since the last two or three years that they brought it to campus. It was to go to Oaxaca, Mexico, for a semester. How I missed my sanctuary of Mexico. I read what it had to say and looked at the pictures. I pinned it to my bulletin board and day-dreamed about it for a while. I figured I would get back to it when the time was right. Maybe it was a calling for me. Each day of the week I filled in a section of the application. I was signing up to go for next year. I prayed that this time next year I would be in Oaxaca. Oddly, this is what got me through the week.

Job had called me earlier on Friday, letting me know that he would pick me up around eight in the evening. So I was pretty surprised that he showed up two hours late.

"Why are you so late?" I asked him very upset.

"Sorry, I got a little caught up," Job apologized.

"You couldn't call me to let me know?" I asked.

"I didn't know I would be this late," he responded.

He was acting a little weird, and I sensed something different about him. "Were you drinking?"

"A little, I'm sorry," he said.

"So where were you?" I asked.

"Just with some of the guys," he said vaguely.

We were driving around for about a half an hour while I interrogated him, trying to figure out what we could do at this hour, since obviously our plans were ruined. "What are we supposed to do now?" I asked still very upset.

"I don't know. I'll see if my friend's restaurant is open," he suggested.

The parking lot was empty. "What did you expect; it's almost midnight," I reminded him.

"It's not that late. We can go to Denny's or IHOP. Wanna go to the city?" he suggested.

"No, Job. Just take me home. I am not in much of a mood to go out with you anymore," I said.

I was glad that things turned out the way they did. Maybe it was God giving me the okay to let him go.

I avoided Job the rest of the weekend. When I got back to school, I took another look at the brochure that read, "Spend a semester abroad in Oaxaca, Mexico." I wanted to go to Oaxaca, but I always had so much fear inside of me. I, like always, still wondered what my parents would say. Would they keep me from broadening my horizons? I thought, what did God want? Maybe this was part of His plan. On Monday morning I turned in the brochure of interested parties to the head of the English and Foreign Language Department. She was excited about me going and said that I would hear from someone in a couple of months, after the final deadline date, to let me know what the next step would be. I felt a little nervous about what I would tell my parents and what it would be like to be that far away from home for so long.

I had a report due for my Roman Catholicism course. We had to pick a topic from the chapter the father assigned us. I chose to do my report on *La Virgen de Guadalupe*. She is an awesome Mexican female icon, with an inspiring and uplifting message. One day she appeared to Juan Diego on his path to Mass, in Tepeyac. She had asked him to be her messenger and speak to the Bishop, requesting the building of a church. But he was shunned, and so felt unworthy of the *Virgen's* choice. The day his uncle fell ill, he raced for a priest, and tried to avoid the *Virgen*, but with her kind words reminded him that she was his loving Mother who offered him protection and comfort. Juan Diego feared rejection by the Bishop, and he feared the loss of his uncle. And what the *Virgen* assured him was that she would be with him to protect him. She healed his uncle and gave him a sign to take to the Bishop. From that point on, that was what I remembered when I feared something. She would protect and comfort me like a caring mother would.

I felt more inspired and no longer afraid about Oaxaca. If anything, I felt excited. I was getting bored already in my environment. It made me wonder if I would feel like this about every place, or if there actually was a place somewhere in this world where I could survive emotionally and spiritually? I was looking forward to a change. I wondered about what kind of job I would have in the future. What would I be able to tolerate? I know school was important, but I also felt trapped by it. I knew it was supposed to be my ticket somewhere, but it had not taken me far yet. Sometimes I wondered if that was part of the reason why I was not that into Job. Would he be boring? Would life with him be the same routine? It did not matter anymore. I was avoiding the ultimate break-up with him, but I knew it had to be done.

I did not have the guts to initiate it so I waited for him to call me, since I knew eventually he would. "Hello," I answered.

"I know you hate me," said Job.

"Of course I don't hate you," I assured him.

"I know I messed up," he said.

"No, you were just doing what you thought was fun. I know I wasn't much fun after a while. I just can't do this with you anymore, Job. I'll be honest, you really did hurt my feelings, and it just made me realize that I can't handle a relationship right now." I told him.

"I'm sorry," he said.

"Don't be. You're a great guy. I guess it is just bad timing for me. I don't want to be distracted from school. Besides, I am actually going to be spending several months in Mexico next year. I definitely can't expect you to wait for me." I told him.

"I would," he said.

"Don't. Take care, Job. Stay in school. Do it for yourself, not for anyone else," I suggested.

"I'll try. You take care, too. Bye," said Job.

I had a strong feeling that Job's life would be filled with much greater blessings beyond what he wanted in me. That weekend I drowned myself back in the sheets of Luke. For one, I knew I would not feel guilty since Job was no longer in the picture. I also knew this time that it was what it was. It seemed as though Luke was always going to be available for me, maybe not emotionally or possibly even spiritually, but he was there. I felt so indifferent, because I knew he was not part of God's plan. I would start to remove myself from Luke emotionally, but now I was hypnotized by him physically. The hard part was dealing with the distance it created between God and me.

When I Feel This Way

My emotions cut through the middle of my existence.

One half floats to the sky—high!
It's wearing Friday night's worst,
with a behavior to match—
and the devil's smile is shining through.
A twinkling eye, a jungle of hair, a laughing piece of heart,
all ready to show just how much they just don't care.

I love it when I feel this way!

The other half crumbles to the ground—like mud and dirt—hurt.
It lies there nude—wet and cold.
Its half of the heart, in a fetal position fold.
A swollen eye, but like an open wound;
feeling the pain of a loveless lover—doomed.

I hate it when I feel this way!

But I live as a whole.
Take all of me—give me all of you.
Intoxicating all night love making—but the morning before,
a love battle, a hate war.

My soul gets ripped in half.
I want to surrender to the Almighty,
ask for forgiveness and make me whole again.
I don't understand it when I feel this way.
What cries of agony make me feel this way?

YZABELLE JIMÉNEZ MARTÍNEZ

Although it was hard to break Job's heart, I was more concerned with my own well being. I was in a state of limbo, confused between God and Luke, cast aside in spiritual purgatory wondering what it would take for me to understand God's plans and expectations. I patiently waited, not for God to extend his hand to me, but for myself to be spiritually willing to return the gesture.

WAITING IN EPHESUS

In him we were also chosen, destined in accord with the purpose of the One who accomplishes all things according to the intention of his will, so that we might exist for the praise of his glory, we who first hoped in Christ.

Ephesians 1:11-12

Once I realized that God did not want me to pursue a committed relationship, I wanted to respect that, but there was one thing getting in the way of that. I figured since I wanted to run off to my sanctuary for a semester anyway in several months, what would be the harm of fitting Luke into my schedule once in a while? I knew what the harm was. It was hurting my relationship with God. But I questioned, did He not want me to have any fun?

One time during confession, a priest asked me what my prayer life was like. I had told him that I went to church every Sunday and prayed at night and in the morning, and sometimes throughout the day as necessary. I listened to Christian radio a lot and had been involved off and on at church. I presently attended a Catholic university and read the Bible sometimes. I prayed the rosary and went to confession. He made me understand that "prayer life" really meant what my relationship with God was like. How do I get to know Him? I suppose through those avenues I was getting to know Him, however, I often felt that God was always in my conscience. On one hand, I had heard His plan that I had to succeed in school and I did move forward with that plan. Yet at times it felt as though I disagreed with Him pertaining to other aspects of my life. Why did I have to give up Luke? There were times when out of spite I tried to push God out of my life, because I felt like He was asking too much of me. We had our disagreements; I knew deep down inside that regardless of what I wanted, eventually God was going to win. It all depended on how long it would take me to return to Him and once again see eye-to-eye with Him. He had a way of hiding in my heart so that I would eventually find my way back to His path and once again be close to Him, but for the time being I had strayed. I would try to focus a lot of time on school. Yet secretly I had my little *rendezvous* with Luke. It was just a secret from my friends, because, of course, God knew. He knows everything.

The moment Job and I were over, Luke was immediately back in my life. I was nearing a birthday. My friends and I from Saint Ambrose were planning a party for me and my roommate, Lily, whose birthday was the day after mine. I had written Luke an invitation asking him to come. The weekend of the party, I went home on Thursday evening for a couple of days, and that was the night that Luke called to let me know that he would not be able to make it, but he would like to celebrate with me that night. Luke came to pick me up and asked me to drive us to his place. It seemed as though nothing mattered anymore in terms of my feelings for him. It became strictly physical. Not that I did not enjoy his company, but I knew that we were not meant to be, that we were not in God's plan. Luke made me feel beautiful and special. It was very easy to be with him. He had no expectations of me. I felt like I could do no wrong in his eyes. I did not want to let go of that feeling. Sometimes it was those encounters that made up for the lack of support that gave me confidence in a different way.

Saturday I returned to school to prepare for my twenty-third birthday party. I had wanted to dedicate this celebration to my brother, Angel. He was killed two weeks before his twenty-third birthday. This celebration was for him. The party was fun. Solomon came. I also snuck away downstairs to the first floor to hang out with a friend that I had made that year, Paul. Paul lived on the co-ed floor of the dorms. He was also older than the traditional college age.

As the semester progressed, a lot was going on in my mind. I was making great waves with the newspaper. There were many people complimenting me on my articles and viewpoints. Yet despite my minor successes, I felt that something was missing in my life, and I was bored. It was purposeless or meaningless or something. I still felt as though what I wanted in life was not clear, or even within reach. Luke was not the problem anymore. I liked Luke and enjoyed the time we spent together, but it was no longer the obsessive longing that it once was. Luke became for me what I was to him. We were just a quick fix to our self-esteem issues, and a pastime for something greater to come in our lives.

I was also spending a lot of time with Solomon. It felt like we had a very intimate friendship, yet he was in a relationship. Spending time with him was not like spending time with other friends, because I had these secret feelings for Solomon. I admired him. I would never act on those feelings though, for many reasons. I was too sensitive to risk any kind of rejection, I respected the fact that he was in a relationship, and I accepted my meaningless relationship with Luke, because I was able to focus more on school. This was my life for a few weeks until spring break came around.

Spring break came early in March and was disappointing because there was a snow storm the weekend I came home, the perks of living in a state with all four seasons. The electricity from miles around was out, including Luke's electricity. He called to let me know that he had no heat, and if I could come and keep him warm. Even though I knew of what our relationship consisted, there were times that I had to convince myself that there was more to it. It was romantic to me that we tried to keep each other warm and entertain ourselves with conversation than always having to have a physical connection.

"So did you get any mail recently?" I asked him this just out of curiosity to see how he would respond.

"No. Why? Did you send me something?" Luke asked.

"No, I thought about it. But I figured that what I wanted to tell you, I should just tell you in person," I said.

"Why? Is it something bad?" he asked.

"No, not really. Not for me," I responded.

"Is it bad for me?" he asked.

"I don't know," I said.

"Well, what?" he questioned impatiently.

"Would you miss me if I were to go away?" I said, continuing to be coy.

"Where would you go?" he asked.

"Mexico," I said.

"You always go to Mexico," he said.

"Yeah, but I'm thinking about going down there for a semester. You know, for school, a study abroad program. Are you gonna miss me?" I asked him.

"Sometimes, I only miss you when you're nice to me."

"I'm not ever not nice to you," I said.

On a few occasions during the break, Judith or my sister and I would go out to the movies and local bars and hangouts to see everyone else that was home for break, or that never went away, because this was the routine of the lost hopes club members. One night Judith, her husband, and I went out to Twister's, and I ran into James. "Hey, Leizel. What's up? How ya doin'?" said James.

"I'm good. How are you? Who are you here with?" I asked out of curiosity.

"Deacon. Why? Did you wanna see Luke?" He asked me.

"No, I was just asking because I see that you're alone," I said.

"Oh, when was the last time you talked to Luke?" James inquired.

"I don't know, why?" I asked defensively.

"Are you guys still talking and seeing each other?" he asked.

"Not really. Why are you asking?" I said, annoyed with Luke.

"I don't know. He told me that he sees you sometimes, like once a week. That you guys still hang out," he replied.

"Oh, yeah?" I said, nonchalantly.

"I mean, I'm not saying anything, I'm just surprised that you're still seeing him," he explained.

I wondered why he was "surprised." Was he judging me? What exactly did he know? What exactly was Luke telling him? I felt pretty embarrassed and could feel the level of my hyper-sensitivity rise. I was okay with how things were between us, because I thought it was solely between the two of us. There was that reappearing taste of dissension brewing within me, anticipating the next conversation Luke and I would have.

Later that week when he called me to "come hang out," I went over to his place in order to have this conversation face-to-face. "I'm glad you called me, Luke," I told him.

"Yeah?" Luke said.

"Yeah, I wanted to ask you something," I said.

"About?" he asked.

"You know how we agreed to have this no-strings attached relationship? Which I also assumed that it would be sort of hush-hush to the public," I said.

"Okay?" He responded, expecting to hear more.

"Is it?" I asked him.

"What do you mean?" He wanted clarification.

"Do you tell your friends about us?" I asked.

"I tell my best friend," he replied.

"James?" I said.

"Yeah, I trust him. I know he isn't gonna tell anyone," he explained.

"I saw him the other day, and he said something to me about us," I informed him.

"Well, you already know." He said with an amusing grin, or so he thought.

"You know what I mean. Now I know that he knows, and that makes me uncomfortable. Do you know how that makes me look? You can't have it both ways. If you don't want a relationship with me, and if I have to settle for whatever this is, then you can't go around telling your friends what is going on between us. That's not fair to me. Do you understand what I mean?"

"Yeah, kind of. It's just hard, because he is my best friend and I tell him everything. Don't you tell Judith everything?" he asked.

"No, sometimes I don't want people to know what I am doing. We agreed that it was going to be between us, and yet you included other people. You made me look bad," I responded.

"Well, I'm really sorry," he said.

After that night, I felt even more disconnected from Luke. I had not wanted to spend time with him, because of how he made me feel. It opened my eyes to the reality of who I was becoming. I was not too proud of it. Luke told me once a while back that I let him off the hook too easy whenever he did anything to hurt me. I always forgave him, made it easy for him to say he was sorry and move on as though nothing had happened, or that everything was fine. This time was different. If he did not realize how much his actions had hurt my feelings, then I was not going to give him another chance to make it up to me. It did not take long for him to call me to see if he had been forgiven.

"Hello," I answered.

"Hey, Leizel," Luke said.

"Hi," I said curtly.

"That's it, a hi? Does this mean that you are still mad at me?" he asked.

"For what?" It was one of those trick questions to see if he knew why he was in trouble.

"I understand why you were upset. It's not like I told him anything personal. I just told him that we hang out and talk and stuff. That you're really cool," he said.

"Well, for my sake, just don't tell anybody anything. Okay? I'm sure he already knows I'm cool," I said jokingly to ease the tension.

He laughed, "You're right. I'm glad you told me this. I won't do it again. Can you come over now?" he asked.

"As long as we have an understanding, I guess." He knew I was being sarcastic, but at the same time he knew that if I had expressed my feelings that I must have been really hurt by it. Confronting him about that whole James incident was not easy for me. Normally I would have acted as though it never even happened.

Plans for Oaxaca were slowly falling into place. During the break I had taken my passport pictures and completed the paper work necessary to turn in to the school. I was also beginning to worry about all the aspects of living in another country for that long. I would miss my family and friends. Would I make new friends? Would I be safe? Comfortable? Happy? Lonely?

I thought about my future again, planning ahead, thinking about a journalism career, or getting certified for teaching high school for a while or getting a master's degree. The one thing I did put out of my thoughts was the distraction of a serious relationship with anyone. I was feeling the pressure of the procrastination of writing essays, reading books, and studying for tests. I was just trying to get through this semester, or at least this week. I was spending time with different people at school, like Solomon. At night I would study with the people that lived in my dorm, such as my roommate Lily, or Paul. I liked Paul because he was centered on his Christian identity, and he was very ambitious. Like Solomon, our friendship was peculiar because he was in a long distance relationship. People would always wonder and comment about how innocent our friendship really was. I respected his relationship. I trusted him to respect me. That was why I chose to spend time with him.

The semester was coming to an end in a few weeks. I had finals to study for and essays to write. I felt the need to avoid Luke. I could tell that he was not in a good place emotionally. As always, I was his safety net, his comfort zone. I made Luke feel good about himself, which I understood, because in the past he had done the same for me. I could no longer spend time worrying about Luke. I had to focus on my present goals.

In addition to catching up with school work, Paul and I hung out together, studying, watching television, and eating lunch together. It had gotten to the point where when my phone rang I wanted it to be Paul wanting to hang out and spend time with me. Like I said, it was not anything romantic. I just felt like Paul liked to be friends with me because of who I was. He was not interested in a physical relationship with me, and that made me feel appreciated. It made me feel that my personality was stronger than my physical beauty, although I wondered if he was attracted to me. I was attracted to his soft brown eyes and caramel skin which made it quite a test to just be friends. I think Paul liked spending time with me, because I respected him, and therefore, in turn, he trusted me. I felt blessed to be able to have made a friendship with someone like him. He wanted to be a gospel musician in order to proudly express his Christian beliefs. I liked that he was goal-oriented, went to church and was very religious. He was getting a degree in education and spent time at the studio. I imagined that he sought my company because he was lonely, yet he must have wanted to feel the same attention that I had wanted. Other times I wondered if he was drawn to me by God, to keep me from making altering mistakes.

Paul made me feel the way that Luke and Job probably felt in comparison to me, that whole, "You make me want to be a better person" theory. It was not that Paul made me "want to be a better person". I did not believe in that idea. I *was* a better person when I was with him, than, say, when I was with Luke. I made better decisions when I was with Paul.

The following weekend I was back with Luke. He seemed confused about the life he had with his feelings for his son's mother, and I was interrupting all of that. I knew he was suffering, but I did not know what was going on in his head, his heart, or his soul. I had stopped seeking Luke, but tried to be available for him when he called. I knew he needed my comfort, and I felt as though I could not abandon him; however, I was finally getting my needs met from other friends in other ways. I know he needed to eventually deal with his problems, but maybe that was why he needed me. I still wrote him a letter every now and then. He needed to feel important, and that was probably why he kept me around. I was okay with that. Even though it was pretty obvious that at this point I was disconnected from God, he was completely removed from God and his religious beliefs.

Another semester had finally come to an end, and I was getting ready for another trip to Mexico with my family. In the meantime, I was spending time with Luke and Solomon. Solomon, at this point, was no longer in a relationship. He had called me a week or so after school was out, and we spent about three hours on the phone talking. I wondered how he felt about me.

We talked mainly like friends. We talked about our relationships. I partly did that so that he would not think I was interested in him. If someone else is in the picture, then it would throw him off the trail of him knowing I had a crush on him. I never wanted him to know. I knew that I did not want to be in a relationship. My heart had been completely closed off to love.

Now that I was home for the summer, Luke would call me on random days and not just on the weekends. Sometimes we talked about whatever was going on with him and his friends or his son, and other times we spent time together. He would ask me to go out to the clubs with him, but I did not feel comfortable being seen with him by people that we knew. We spent more time together again, and I could see an improvement in his demeanor. I went back and forth from Luke to Solomon, although Solomon and I had a strictly innocent friendship. Phoebe had graduated from college, and Solomon had come over. We had a celebration for her at the park, but by the time Solomon showed up, it was already over. We hung out on the porch since it was a hot summer's night and talked for hours. He had cut his Jesus-like hair, but he was still cute. He left around midnight and told me to give him a call when I got back from Mexico.

In mid-June, my family and I headed to Mexico. It had gotten to the point where when I was there for the two weeks with my parents and family, not much was happening. Hannah was at school in another little town about two hours away from Sayula. I did not have many friends to spend time with in Sayula. I did not want to stay longer than the two weeks, as I usually did, because there was not much for me to do. I did run into Alejandro, and he had asked me to meet him in the *centro* for lunch. We walked around the garden area. It was traditional for the male to walk on the outside of a female. It was a cultural symbol of protection, but of course I saw it as a male machismo form of possession. After fifteen minutes of getting him to see it my way, he let me walk on the outside, despite the stares we received. We talked a lot about the typical political topics we had in the past and played a few games of air hockey in the local arcade. Over the weekend I went to the club at which he worked, and we spent some time together there as well. We exchanged e-mails and agreed to keep in touch.

Returning from Mexico always gave me a few days to think about what I wanted to get back to in my life in Illinois. After a few days, I had called Luke to see how he was these days, but he was not home. I did not have the strength to let him go.

One mid-July weekend, I had gone to Judith's to watch a movie. It had been a while since we caught up on all our gossip, she about married life and children, and I about the potpourri of who was meant for me. Later that night when I got home, Luke called me. "What are you doing?" He asked immediately.

"I just got home," I answered.

"From where?" he asked.

"Hanging out with Judith. Why? What are you doing?" I asked.

"I was just thinking about you. Missing your kisses," he replied charismatically.

I always wondered if he was drunk or sober. "Well, that's your fault," I said.

"I know. You're right. I should be spending more time with you. It's easy to be with you. You're so nice, sometimes. It's like a getaway," he said.

"Wow, really? It doesn't feel like that for me." I said, surprised by his compliment.

"I know. But come over anyway. I miss you. Are you gonna come?" he insisted.

"Yeah. I'll be there in about ten minutes," I said.

During the week I received a letter from school asking me to be a peer mentor for the six-week course that helps prepare incoming freshmen to meet the challenges of a four-year university. It was a nice honor to be able to take on this new position at school. I had to do an interview, and if I did well, I had to do a two or three-day training session. Mrs. Kyria was the one that recommended me for the position. She was my teacher when I had to take this course. I liked this recognition. It gave me hope. It gave me satisfaction about who I was. It gave me confidence and pride. On Friday I went to the interview, and everything went well. It was more of a formality than anything else.

Although things were going well for me, professionally, I was still having a hard time emotionally and spiritually. I kept going through this yo-yo phase of shutting down and isolating myself. I was now the one with the huge intimacy and commitment issues. I did not trust anyone, and I did not know if I ever would. I did not like opening up about my feelings. I did not like people belittling what was important to me or judging and criticizing me. I did not want people to tell me what I should do or what I should not do. I did not want people to tell me how I should feel or live my life. I longed for the courage to be able to be open and trust someone. I longed to be able to find someone that would not judge me or tell me how to live my life. I longed for support and acceptance of who I was and what I wanted, regardless of what other people wanted for me. I longed for protection and comfort, but I no longer had that. I know I was looking for that comfort in all the wrong places, which was why I was not finding it.

I knew that I was disconnected from God, but I also felt like, without school, what was I supposed to be doing? School was the plan, the goal and passion. It was a sense of guidance for me. That was also why I felt lost. I needed to get through a few more weeks before school started, and I could feel like I had a sense of purpose again. Then I began to worry. I was not going to be in school forever. What was I meant to do once school was over? Do I wait around for God to send me a ray of hope, or is God waiting for me to find my own ray of hope and follow Him down the right path?

The last two weeks before school, I busied myself as much as I could for them to go by fast. I had spent a few days training for the teacher's assistant position. Luke and I spoke on the phone a few times, but I no longer had the desire to see him. There were times when I would call, and then there were times that he would call and ask to see me. I would make up some excuse to not spend time with him. It was like I was finally looking for something more. I knew my feelings for him would never lead to giving me a purpose or help me discover what I had been searching for to feel complete.

Soon enough it was the first day of school again. It was funny how indifferent I had felt about school. I wanted to get on with my educational plan, but I felt so emotionally disconnected, not wanting to associate with many people. I had the desire to spend lots of time alone. I busied myself with school responsibilities and felt overwhelmed. I also knew that this would be my toughest semester until I was ready to graduate. I used my busy schedule as an excuse to avoid people. The person I saw the most was Lily, and that was only because she was still my roommate. By the end of the first week, many of my friends had complained to me about how withdrawn I seemed. I would sarcastically apologize for my busy schedule of five classes, the newspaper, tutoring, and being a teacher's aide. Oh, yeah, and I would remind them that I also had to eat and sleep, and ask them to please forgive me for that.

Paul and I had a disagreement, because he felt that I was always busy before, yet we always had time for each other. So I tried to make more time for him, seeking him in his room and calling him. There were times when he was also very busy, spending a lot of time at the studio, student teaching, and preparing for graduation. When I brought attention to his busy schedule, it was not the same thing. It made me realize how even the nice guys expect you to meet their needs, but yet they do not feel responsible for helping meet your needs. It made me feel as though I would never fall in love, because there does not exist the perfect man. At least, the perfect man for me did not exist. Then there was always Solomon, who looked out for me and listened to me. Ironically, I thought Solomon was the perfect man for someone, just not for me. He would visit me once in a while when I was in the tutoring center. He was very considerate, asking me if I had already had lunch and if I wanted him to bring me anything. He passed by quite often, because the graphic design and art department were in the same wing as the writing center. I used Solomon as a symbol of hope that the perfect man, or that a good man did exist for me. I did not want to get too close to him, because I did not want him to ruin that fantasy for me.

I immersed myself in my school responsibilities in order to avoid feelings that were uncertain. The first newspaper of the year was coming out, and I was pretty excited about that. When it did come out, I received many compliments on my articles. That was one of the major highlights of my semester. In addition to the confidence the newspaper was giving me, I was preparing for my study abroad program in January. Besides the teacher's aide position, there was nothing new about this semester, just different classes and different professors. I lived through this semester very remotely. I wanted to find a new part of my life and myself, yet I wanted to find the old part of my life that once belonged to God. I saw Luke one last time before I left the country and let him know that it would be a while before we saw each other again. I had hoped the best for him and that he would find what he needed in God. All I could do was to pray for him.

I Pray for You Every Night

In my prayers, I whisper your name
asking God to not only ease your pain,
but to guide and help you find the right of way,
and to fulfill your idea of happiness every day.

I ask that God give you the strength needed to carry through
life's decisions that are best for you.
He shows you faith and believes in you
so you believe in yourself and have faith in Him, too.

I ask that He reward you for the special time you share
with a small, blessed loved one for whom you are destined to care.
Just before I cross myself and dream the night away,
I thank Him on my behalf for sending you my way.

And despite the path of our destiny,
you will always remain special to me.

In my mind, I had hoped that this getaway was what I needed to be able to forget about Luke and be able to move on with God's plan. Solomon and I had agreed to keep in touch through e-mail, as many of my friends and family had agreed to do. More than anything, I had the biggest disconnection from God. I was ready to find myself. I was ready to figure out what it was that I wanted in life, to find my way back to God's plan, all of His plan, whole-heartedly, and finally to find my way back to God. I could not believe how lost I was. I was ready for what I needed to find in my sanctuary. And, of course, the rebuilding of mine and God's relationship always started with penance. It was my way of reaching back to God and let Him know that I was sorry and I was back.

FREED BY
GOD'S DECREE

But the Lord said, "I have witnessed the affliction of my people in Egypt and have heard their crying of complaint against their slave drivers, so I know well what they are suffering….What sort of thing is this that you are doing for the people?"…The people come to me to consult God…. They come to me to have me settle the matter…and make known to them of God's decisions and regulations.

Exodus 3:7, 18:14-16

I liked that I was going away in the beginning of the year. I had this lame tradition that every year before the end of an old year and at the start of the New Year, I would say good-bye to the significant people and events in my life that were gone, but also give thanks to all the new blessings that came along that year. On New Year's Day, I picked a theme for the upcoming year, a theme that was reflective of the kind of life that I wanted to live that year. I would propose all the challenges that I would have to meet in order to make the theme of my new year happen.

I was grateful for my old friends like Judith and Hannah; I was happy for Judith's new life. I was grateful for my friends from Saint Ambrose, Lily, Paul, Solomon, and the girls from the dorm. I knew that I would be saying good-bye to Job, and deep down inside, I knew it was time to say good-bye to Luke. This year's theme was going to be: Hope and Appreciation. I wanted to be able to do more for the people I cared about and give more support to the causes that were meaningful to me. I wanted to invest all my hope and faith in the Lord. There was so much for which I was praying and hoping in my life. I hoped the experience of living in Oaxaca would be life changing. I hoped that I would get into a good graduate school. I hoped that I would find someone that would love me the way I wanted and deserved to be loved, and lastly I hoped that I would find God.

Although I had been building up my desire to go away to Oaxaca, I had never been away from home for more than two or three months at a time. I was afraid to leave the comfort and security of my parents' love. Judith spent hours on the phone convincing me that everything would be okay. I debated changing my mind, but I remembered that if this was what God wanted, just like Diego, I had no need to fear anything with the protection of *La Virgen de Guadalupe*. I had to trust God's will and know that He would take care of me.

The night before I left, there was a snow storm. The area around our car needed serious shoveling. The roads had not been salted yet. My father was trying to convince me to stay. I know that he did not want me to go, but I felt as though this was the next step in God's plan for me. My mother helped me shovel the car free and then decided to just drive me to the closest Holiday Inn, where a scheduled bus would take us to the airport. She rode with me all the way to the airport to say good-bye. The storm caused my flight to be delayed several hours.

Soon enough, though, I was beginning the New Year in a new place, and I would begin a new life. My classes were Monday, Wednesday, and Friday, and other than that, I had no idea what would become of the rest of my time in Oaxaca. It took a while for me to accept all the changes. I was nervous about being in this unfamiliar place, alone, far away from everything I knew. I made a commitment that I had to complete, no matter how bad the experience would be. I wondered what would happen day by day. How would I adjust? What would this experience bring me? What did God have in store for me?

The first few days were hard, because I had to be alone and do everything by myself. I was afraid to be in this unknown world by myself. It made me realize how protected I was by my parents and how my family had always been around me. I know sometimes we need our alone time, a break from those people that are constantly in our presence; because they are always there, we take for granted that they will continue to always be there.

For the first several weeks, I stayed in a hotel. I did not like the fact that it was not a real home, a place where I could make food and feel as though I had a sense of privacy and comfort. Food is always a symbol of home, especially in the Mexican culture. I did not like that it felt like a place where I was being monitored all the time. I did not like someone coming into my room every day, sometimes waking me up just to make the bed. So needless to say, this was going to be a temporary situation.

My first discouraging experience was going into a bakery. I grabbed a pair of tongs and a tray to get ready to make my picks of delicious sweet breads, cakes, and cookies. As I started to place a piece of dark chocolate cake on my tray, it had fallen onto the floor. I was not very good at using the bread tongs. A worker came out to clean it up, but she yelled at me. She said I was careless and that I would be charged for my "stupid mistake." I remembered the time when I was in Sayula and my father was going to go to the bakery. He asked me what I wanted, and I told him that all I wanted was a pineapple *empanada*. When he came back, he had three bags of sweet bread. One of those bags was filled with nothing but pineapple *empanadas*. In that short period of a time I missed my parents and appreciated even the little things they did for me. I would never have treated anyone that meanly over fifty cents, which was the equivalent of the five *pesos*. In addition to the natives, the American tourists in this place are overabundant. Some of them are somewhat rude as well. I wondered what could have happened in their life that they ran away from their own country to live here. All I could do was hope it would get better.

Before the rest of the students got there, I had been spending time with my Spanish teacher from Saint Ambrose who was in charge of overseeing the project at the university. She had only planned to be there for a few days before school began back in Chicago and asked me if I wanted to accompany her to all the ancient ruins. The most well known ruins in Oaxaca are Monte Alban and Mitla. They are both pre-Columbian archaeological sites. One thing I noticed about Oaxaca that was very different from northern Mexico was that there was so much history and culture. Maybe I just noticed it more because it was so different from the northern Mexico I knew. When I go to Jalisco, I spend time with family and friends, and it is all I really know, so it never seemed like a place of tourism for me.

Last semester, only four women came for the program. This semester the same four women returned because they liked it so much. They were all older than me, and so I was not sure how much I would have in common with them. I was the only new student joining them this semester. Because I was on an advanced Spanish track, I took three classes and was required to do field work. And since Saint Ambrose was a Catholic school, there was a requirement to serve the community in some way as a volunteer. The courses I took were a Mexican art class, an anthropology class on the culture of the indigenous peoples of Oaxaca, and lastly, a Spanish language conversation class. The fieldwork required me to visit a pre-school located in a city on the outskirts of Oaxaca. Guillermo Gonzalez Guardado was a city for one of Oaxaca's municipal dumping grounds. I volunteered through the lending library. Many parts of Mexico are not familiar with the idea of borrowing books for a few weeks and then returning them. The lending library wanted to expand on the idea by donating children's books to schools in small towns and sending people out to teach the children how to use and care for books. So I was that person. I chose and purchased the books to bring with me, read them to the children, and developed activities related to the context that would help them with their motor skills. Classes were an hour and a half long. They were all on the same days so that those of us with fieldwork were able to have flexible schedules to go and volunteer on our free days. It was hard not having something to do all the time. If you recall the schedule I once led: classes, volunteer work, newspaper, tutor, teacher's aide. I was very driven, and now I had nowhere to drive.

Once I found out what my fieldwork would be, I visited different book stores to get ideas as to what I could do. However, the president of the library was out of town and I had to meet with her before I could begin. One of the other students, Raquel, took me under her wing. She was about twenty years older than me and was essential in me getting comfortable and meeting other people. She showed me around, took me to all the hot spots, and introduced me to a few other people. The most common place where she and the other ladies went to was an Italian restaurant, mostly specializing in pizza, called El Refugio. As soon as we sat down, I felt a lot of heavy stares, and the waiter immediately came to attend us. Raquel came here often, but more often than her, Marilyn came here. Marilyn was another woman that came back for a second semester. She was in her mid-thirties. She was a religious attendee of El Refugio.

"Hey Raquel, who is this?" the waiter asked.

"Neftali, this is Leizel. She is a new student," Raquel responded.

He grabbed my hand to greet me. "Are you from Chicago, too?" Neftali asked.

"Yes," I answered.

Before I left, Neftali had offered to show me around, and I let him. We had agreed to meet at the Santo Domingo Museum at ten in the morning on Tuesday. As Raquel saw us make plans, she was a little skeptical. "Are you going out with him?" she asked.

"He offered to show me around," I said.

"Just be careful," she warned me.

"What do you mean? Why?" I asked, concerned.

"Marilyn might not like it," she replied.

"Why? What does she care? Are they dating?" I inquired.

"She thinks so," Raquel said.

"What?" I asked, confused.

"She has a huge crush on him. According to her, they dated for quite some time a few months ago. She has said some crazy things that went on between them. The only thing is that no one has ever seen them together and no one really knows if it is true," Raquel explained.

"Do you think it's true?" I asked.

"Not really, but she really seems to believe it," said Raquel.

"But they are obviously not together right? Otherwise he wouldn't be asking me out," I said.

"Well they're not together, no, but you still need to be careful once she finds out," she warned.

"What's she gonna do? Kill me, or just like cry a little?" I said, sarcastically.

I was only twenty-three at the time and seeing as this Marilyn woman was ten years older than I was, I kind of felt sorry for her. I wanted to go out with him because I wanted to have things to do, but I also did not want to seem selfish and inconsiderate, even though I did not even know this woman. I did not want to rule out the idea of going out with him without getting to know him. If I chose not to see him, I wanted it to be because I made the decision. I wanted it to be because he was not right for me and not because of someone trying to control people's destinies. Unfortunately, the date never even happened. Everything was so new and I could not believe how naïve I was to it all.

Monday after class, Raquel told me that on Saturday they went to El Refugio and Neftali was gone. He left to go back to Veracruz, where he was from originally, because he was just not happy in Oaxaca. I know what it is like to be away from home and your family. The one thing that I had to get used to was being alone. Perhaps learning to be physically alone, but not feeling emotionally lonely, was a characteristic that God needed me to possess. "Raquel, who told you this?" I asked her.

"The guys from the restaurant. They said he just left. He didn't tell you anything?" answered Raquel.

"No, he didn't," I said.

Wednesday after class Raquel and I went to El Refugio and to my surprise Neftali was there.

Raquel immediately excused herself to the restroom. "Leizel, what happened to you?" asked Neftali.

"What happened to you? Raquel told me that all the guys told her you left, and moved back to Veracruz," I said.

"I called off, but I didn't go anywhere. I was sick. Stomach flu. They were probably just messing with her. You can't believe anything these guys say. You have to trust me. If I told you to meet me, then you should have met me," he said.

"Did you show up?" I asked.

"Yes, and I waited and waited and waited," he replied.

"I'm sorry. I thought you had left," I explained.

"So what? Can we try this again?" he asked.

"Yes. Well, I'm really sorry," I said.

"How about Friday, nine in the morning, in the *zocalo*. We'll have breakfast," suggested Neftali.

"That's fine." It really was not fine. I hated getting up early, especially when I had the choice. As we were leaving he grabbed my hand and pulled me close to kiss me on the cheek. I felt a little embarrassed. I felt like, hey, guy, what are you doing? So many people were around, and we had barely met. We had not even had our first date. I guess it was just culturally customary. Mexicans were very affectionate.

Later that night I could not help but think about Luke. I am not sure how I was feeling about him. It had only been several weeks that I had been gone, but I was trying hard to make some kind of a busy life for myself that now I wanted to slow down and think about what I left behind. I knew I had to let go, although at times I felt like I had to be there for him when he needed me. I wished him well. I prayed for him to be happy and that one day he would be at peace with his struggle for happiness. I also prayed that I would one day be at peace with him not being in my life.

I woke up around eight to get ready to meet Neftali. He was about fifteen minutes late. At first I thought that he was not going to show, but eventually he did. After we ate, we went to Santo Domingo church, where we were supposed to have met the last time. Santo Domingo is both a church and a museum.

"This is one of the churches I have been coming to," I said.

"Why way out here?" Neftali asked.

"Because it's big and pretty," I responded.

"So you're Catholic?" he asked.

"Yes. Are you?" I asked.

"No. I haven't really identified with a religion for a while. I don't see the point." I just smiled. I do not know if this is where I was supposed to convince him that religion was important, or if I was supposed to be shocked that he did not have a religious label. I definitely knew that I did not feel spiritually prepared to convince people about God and about being a Catholic at this point in my life. I was barely beginning to learn about who I was. So he left a pause, and since I did not chime in to lecture him on that, he went on about his beliefs. "Don't get me wrong, I know that I believe in God. I just think that the Catholic religion has too many contradictions," he said. Again, I was not sure how to debate about all this. I think what people do not understand is that a religion is not contradictory; it is some of the people that follow it. They are the ones that are claiming to believe in one thing yet living their life in another way, and all the while they are not doing anything to try and change for the better or repent any of their actions.

They say that the three things you should never talk about at a party in order to avoid confrontation are religion, politics, and sex. I do not know if that applies on a first date, but the next topic of discussion was politics. He mentioned the present economical crises of his country, the lack of real governmental leadership, and the poor state of education. He reminded me a little of Alejandro, the only difference was that Alejandro's interests and judgments were followed by actions. He was in college learning all about politics and how to legally change and help his country and fellow citizens. What was Neftali doing? He was serving pizza. He was obviously a very opinionated man, and he must have wanted me to think him intriguing. I listened to him, as most men want a woman to do, especially on their first date. Mainly I do this to feel out the guy and honestly, I listen because I do not want to talk about myself. When he did expect me to talk, I mostly talked about school and my family.

In the back of my mind I wondered about him and Marilyn. I wondered what had happened between them and how accurate it would be according to her story. Only, I felt like it was too soon to ask him about something he could lie about. It is helpful to see how often a man lies, what he lies about, and how well he does it, so when you get to a point in your relationship where a significant question has to be asked, you will know how trustworthy he is. Do not get me wrong, I am not saying that all men lie, but a great deal of people in general lie, even women. I know I have. Aside from not wanting to hurt people's feelings, I know I do it because I do not want to appear vulnerable at times. Men rarely want to seem to appear vulnerable, so lying appeals more to their lifestyle. One thing I did know was that I seemed to be into men with great depth or complexity, and Neftali was no different. I also knew that he was in my path for a reason, but it would not be a very long journey, and I was interested in knowing what purpose we would serve for God and each other.

Later that evening Raquel had made plans to meet at El Refugio. When I showed up to the restaurant, she was not there, but Marilyn was. I felt uncomfortable being alone with her. Mainly because I did not know her that well, and I felt weird about dating the guy whom she "supposedly dated" and with whom she may still "be in love." We talked; I was the one that listened to her. She told me about how at one point in her life she was in a doctoral program at some school in Virginia. It was a master's/doctorate program that she never finished. She dropped out and went back to Chicago and started a master's program at Saint Ambrose. In addition to our conversation, we ate and had a few beers. As we were getting ready to leave, she excused herself to the restroom, and that was when Neftali made his way toward my table.

"What are you gonna do right now?" Neftali asked.

"I don't know. We're getting ready to leave here," I said.

"Let's go out, to a club or bar or something," he suggested.

"What about Marilyn? Should I ask her to come along?" I asked.

"We're going out on a date. I want to be alone with you. We don't need her tagging along," he said.

I wondered what he was thinking about her. I could not picture them together. Marilyn was this very skinny lady with fake blonde hair. She actually looked older than she was, but acted like she was younger. She was almost ten years older than Neftali. He, on the other hand, was very dark, almost purple. He had dark wavy hair, dark thick eye lashes, and very full lips. But he was also slender, and so the shape of his face revealed a chiseled bone structure. Marilyn was a little goofy, and Neftali was fun, but more smart and serious. I wondered how well they communicated. She did not speak Spanish very well, and he did not speak English very well.

"What am I supposed to tell her?" I asked Neftali.

"Just leave and come back," was his solution. I knew in the back of my mind that he did not want her to know that I was going out with him. That should have made me suspicious, but at the time it had never occurred to me. If she was kind of not all there, just what was she capable of doing in a situation about which she might not be too pleased? Marilyn seemed to have slipped in quietly as Neftali was walking away. She had a very curious look on her face. "What did he say to you?" she asked me.

"He asked if we were leaving now. I said yes, we were, because we were kind of tired," I said.

"Are you sure that was all he said?" she asked.

"Yeah," I responded.

"Okay, I just want to make sure he isn't asking you out, so I can just forget about him," she informed me.

As we both left the booth and headed out the restaurant, I kept the conversation about Neftali going. "What do you mean forget about him?"

"We dated for several months, and it was very hot and heavy," she said about the relationship.

"Hot and heavy!" I did not know people talked like that any-more, but that was all she told me. I was curious about whether they had something going on or not, mainly because they were just so different. Clearly if they did date, it seemed like he was over it and had moved on from whatever they were doing. I thought about what Raquel told me, how she thought nothing happened between them, and it all just happened in Marilyn's mind. I felt guilty about lying to her. I did not want to hurt her feelings. I also felt guilty because she was a woman. I hated to see women backstab each other, and I would never want to appear like that was what I was doing to her. We walked together for a few minutes, and then we parted ways. Luckily she lived in the opposite side of town from where I lived. We were right by the *zocalo,* so I waited there for a few minutes, and then I went back to the restaurant. I waited for Neftali to get off work. We roamed around the town. He wanted to take me to a small bar where he used to bartend. They were showing this movie, *Kids.* I was not familiar with it, but it is about kids from ages twelve to seventeen who live a fast life of sex, drugs, alcohol, stealing, and violence, and the harsh consequences of it all. In other words, they did not have Jesus in their life. Ironically, at the end, Jesus Christ is men-tioned, which gives hope in the future for the youth that maybe Christ is an afterthought of such destructions of sin. Maybe that was the message.

"Have you ever seen this movie before?" Neftali asked me.

"No, I have never even heard of it," I responded.

"It's about these young kids who grow up way too fast. You know, doing drugs and having sex. I like it, because I can relate to it. What kind of drugs have you done?" He asked very casually.

"None! I never felt the need to. I'm guessing you have?" I responded.

"Well yeah, it was the only way to survive," he told me.

"Survive what?" I asked.

"Being alone, raising myself. My dad left and came back and left and came back and left. Every time he left, my mom took it out on me. She said it was my fault. Sometimes she would leave for days at a time, too. I was only like eight years old. She would bring in all these other men for a night or two and then leave again. I had to steal to survive and I had to find ways for money. When I got older I ran away, at like twelve, and then I was living in the streets, and then I had to survive that life," he explained.

"Well, that movie is not my reality. It might be like that for some people, but I have never felt like that," I said.

"You are well protected from that reality. I can sense a lot of fear in you because of it," he said.

"Well, it's not like that life is hard to come by. I was blessed with parents who were good examples of living a healthy and happy life. You were not, and so you felt that since no one cared about you, you would live a reckless life in hopes that someone would care." I ignored the "fear in you" part! I also summed him up to see how he would like it!

"I know I love my mother, but I don't think I could ever forgive her for not giving me what I needed as a child," he said.

Again, I was grateful for having parents that tried to protect me from that type of reality. I had a different reality. My reality was my family, education, and Christ. I know he felt like I had it easy, but I did not. Some people think it is just easy to give up on life, run away, and live on the streets. Others cannot even fathom how hard it must be to have that kind of life, to give up all together on the blessings that one could have, and accept to have nothing. And what about one's teenage life? It is a tender age to feel that no one cares what would happen to them. Jesus cares. It is never as bad as it seems. There is always someone there to help; it may not be a family member, but it is a brother or sister in Christ.

As far as Neftali was concerned, I could sense he felt lonely. He had a lot of anger and resentment inside that was holding him back from doing greater things for himself and for God. Forgiveness is a very challenging virtue. It was not healthy for him to horde all this unresolved anger in his soul. How would God cleanse his soul from the poisons of pain and hostility if he did not allow himself to forgive or accept the forgiveness of others?

After we left the bar, we walked all the way up the auditorium stairs where the *Guelaguetza* celebrations took place. It is located on top of a hill, at approximately five thousand feet in altitude. From the top of all the steps, we took in a bird's eye view of the entire city at three in the morning. I was both speechless and breathless by the time I got all the way up the steps. Below was the city, above were the stars and a beautiful dark night sky. We sat quietly on a ledge and let what looked like the entire world, get soaked up by our hypnotic stares. I know I was also doing a lot of reflection on the conversation we had. Neftali put his arms around me. My back was to him, and he grabbed my hands.

"You're hands are cold," he said. I allowed him to warm them. We stood up after twenty minutes and began our journey back down the steps. In the middle of each set of steps there were little balconies where people could stand and look down to take pictures or take breaks if they got tired. I walked over to a balcony to continue looking down, and that was when Neftali kissed me. I have had a few great first kisses, but his was different. I remember Luke's kisses were always passionate and very embracing. Neftali's kiss was so sincere, like he had been waiting since the moment he saw me to give me that kiss; the passion of that kiss was meant only for me. As he was kissing me, he held me very close and very tight.

I thought of the story, *Aladdin*. Walking up and down the auditorium stairs, and then walking home, I felt like the princess and that he was Aladdin. I felt like I had been out of my palace walls and he was showing me his way of life. He was the one with all the street smarts from growing up poor. He was exposing me to his world, and I was hearing about a life I could have never even imagined. He was right, though; there was a bit of fear in me being out at this hour in a place with which I was not that familiar, even though I was with him. Neftali felt safe and comfortable showing me around in his world and demonstrating to me all the knowledge he possessed, despite his lack of institutional education. He had been fending for himself for a long time. I knew why God put him in my path, and I knew that God would soon take him out. So the only goal I had was to serve God by listening for His plan of action to help Neftali.

When I got home, before I went to bed, I reflected on another aspect of this whole, "there is fear in you" comment, but in a different light than being afraid of his unsafe world. I was afraid, afraid of love, being loved. So he was right. He said that the things I feared were due to being sheltered and overprotected by my parents, but on the contrary, the fear existed from taking risks and being vulnerable by allowing people into my heart at moments when I was not being protected. When my guard, or my parents' guard was down, people would hurt me. That was the only fear within me. Neftali and I made plans to meet at the church again on Tuesday at ten in the morning.

After three weeks of living in the hotel, I was ready to find something new. Saturday morning I went to go see a room on the other side of town, closer to where Marilyn lived. I liked the room and its amenities. Martha was the woman that was in charge of renting the rooms in the house. She did not own the house, but she kept it up for an old woman that could not maintain it herself. She was an American woman originally from Boston. She was also about twenty years older than me, but she did not look it. The house was two stories. At the entrance was the kitchen, to the right was the dining room and a living room where she kept her keyboard and piano. All the way in the back was a separate room from the house. That was Martha's room. Up the stairs were four bedrooms and a bathroom that she rented to mostly tourists. I had told Martha that I wanted one of the bedrooms and that I would have first month's rent for her by next Saturday. Basically this meant that I had to let my parents know. So I told them about the place and they agreed to front me the money. I usually worked several jobs on campus to make the extra money that I needed, but in this case I was not allowed to work. I was also going to Mass every Sunday, and before I went out every evening. In addition, in return for God's shelter and protection since my parents were not around, I sacrificed meat the whole time I was there. I felt God's presence in my life again, and I did not want to do anything to feel disconnected from Him anymore. I needed Him to watch over me.

Neftali and I went out three or four times a week for the next couple of weeks, sometimes in the day before I had class and he had work, and sometimes at night after he got off work. Often times I would go to the restaurant where he worked with the girls from class, and when I went downstairs to the restroom he would wait for me outside to talk and surprise me with a kiss or hug. He helped me move all my belongings into my new place. The thing I liked about the new place was that Martha let me use her computer to check and send e-mail. I had barely been communicating with my friends and family from home. I was looking forward to sitting down and having some quality e-mail time.

On one of our dates, Neftali had taken me to a natural park up the hills in San Felipe del Agua. It was absolutely breathtaking. I liked it mainly because I love to be near God's natural resources. I was climbing these huge rocks, jumping over water springs and creeks, and walking along dirt roads. Although I liked it and it was a very beautiful experience, I wish I had known what to expect. I was not dressed for the occasion. I was wearing a little dress, so I was practically eaten alive by all these bugs. I was wearing sandals with my bare feet, and when I jumped from one rock to another I landed on a huge rock under a puddle and made a nice size gash in my skin. I did not complain, though. I did not tell him that I was hurt. There was not anything he could do. I did not want to leave. I wanted to tough it out. We used some of that romantic scenery to make out a little. After that date I could tell that he wanted a more serious relationship, but I did not. I prayed that night for the Lord to give me strength to fight any temptation and let me know what His plan for me was to help Neftali.

I know God was using me as an instrument, because I had to convince Neftali that he was special and that God loved him. God wanted a relationship with him through Jesus. Something I had noticed about Neftali after having spent so much time with him were the scars on his wrist. I never asked him about them, but I knew at one point he had hated himself or his life so much that he did not want to live, and God was using me to show him how much He did love him and how much He could improve his life if he allowed himself a relationship with God. I was willing to help him, which was why he and I needed to continue this pure relationship.

Through all this time Neftali and I were spending together, eventually Marilyn found out that we were dating from one of his co-workers. She had confronted me about it, and I told her that it was true. She told me too much information about their relationship that I did not want to know, and I still thought about what Raquel said. I did not want to feel like I had to choose between her friendship and dating him. I was friends with both of them for a reason. God wanted me to show Neftali how much he was loved and appreciated, and I believed that Marilyn needed something from me, too. I did not want her to be sad, though. She was crying when I told her the truth, and she was crying throughout all the specific details of what they did. I do not necessarily mean sexual details, but specific details. She was so specific in telling me descriptions of actions and words and how he did or said something. It was hard to imagine that the stories she was telling me could have only happened in her imagination. They were very vivid and detailed. I do not even know what the big deal was. Both of them were contemplating leaving Oaxaca, anyway. Marilyn had planned on going back to Chicago, because she was not doing anything here. She could not afford school anymore and had dropped out of Saint Ambrose. Neftali had been talking about going to New Jersey. He said he had a cousin there and he wanted to be around family.

Aside from classes, dating Neftali and going out and getting to know Oaxaca with the few friends I had, I felt like I needed more professional stimulation, especially after the Program Coordinator from my school brought in a few copies of the university newspaper. First of all, there was some other girl's name next to the editor position that I used to have. And second of all, this girl plagiarized one of my prize-winning introductions from an article I had written about a professor that had passed away. I worked hard on that introduction, and she stole it from me and took credit for it like nothing.

I missed writing. Martha, the woman who was renting to me, was telling me about this tourist newspaper that published in English and that I should talk to the editor about letting me write for her. So I went to talk to her. We brainstormed some ideas of what I could write. The newspaper was only published once a month and so at least for these few months that I would be here, I could write an article a month. It was just a volunteer position, but the point was to be able to do some writing and get bylines for a portfolio. My assignment was to research and write about non-profit organizations that benefited the poverty-stricken children of Oaxaca.

Finally, I met the library president and was able to begin my fieldwork. I had asked permission to do my first article on the library and the new program that the library was implementing in the schools. Most of the places I researched just wanted to get people's attention for monetary donations, and for them to volunteer their time to help the organizations. The newspaper was geared toward the American/European tourists of Oaxaca.

A few of the people from the lending library and my program coordinator accompanied me to the pre-school at which I would be volunteering. By early February I was situated with my three classes, my fieldwork position, my volunteer writing, and my new home. I had set up my volunteer hours to go to the pre-school on Tuesdays and Thursdays from ten to one. Soon enough I was beginning to have a satisfying experience.

After I was settled in my new room, the first thing I did was check my e-mail. It had been awhile so I had several messages; five were from Solomon. He was asking how everything was going and how he missed hanging out with me. I wrote him back telling him about my fieldwork and the articles I would be writing. I did not tell him about Neftali. Neftali had missed the last two dates we arranged. I had not been in his restaurant in almost a week. I felt bad that he stood me up and that he had not made any efforts to correct his mistake, but I was also a little relieved because he was trying to move faster than I had wanted.

Our anthropology teacher took us on an all day excursion one Sunday. We visited four historic places. Our first stop was a sixteenth-century church located in the city of Tlacochahuaya. The city is also known for its exquisite cuisine and marketplace. We visited three ruins, Dainzu, Lambityeco, and Yagul. Yagul was my favorite of the three. There we got to climb mountains, which was something I had never done before. It was very invigorating to me. I had never experienced so many adventures with nature in general until I had come to Oaxaca. I felt very spiritually connected to God by being within His natural resources. Monday morning before class, I had gotten up early to check my e-mail. I heard a knock, and when I answered the door, there was Neftali and his explanation.

"Hi. Come in, I was just checking my e-mail." I did not know if I should be upset with him or not.

"How have you been? Sorry about missing our dates. I was sent to food courses for the restaurant for the past two or three days. And I had to work on Wednesday, so they gave me today off. So look, that's why I am here today. Why haven't you been to the restaurant?" Neftali said.

I had been looking at the computer screen the whole time he had been talking to me, so I turned in his direction and said, "Because I didn't want to see you. I was upset with you." Then I looked back at the screen.

"Well, I'm sorry, but it wasn't my fault." I looked back at him when he said this and so he followed by saying, "It isn't your fault, either."

"It's fine. I understand," I said.

"Well, will you at least go with me to get something to eat so we can talk? I haven't eaten yet," he said.

Neftali and I went to the restaurant across the street from the house. I had a busy day of classes, picking up books for my field work, and working on my first article ahead of me. He walked me back across the street but did not walk me all the way to the door. I told him that I would stop by the restaurant later in the week so we could go out after he got off work. I did not tell him exactly when though; I was being coy with him. I thought I would make him anticipate the next time we saw each other. Besides, I was beginning to lose interest in him. He kept mentioning how he was going to leave, and frankly, I did not want the same thing he wanted anymore from this relationship. However, I still felt like God needed me to stay in his life for a little longer, which I was willing to do.

That is the week I started my fieldwork with the kids from the pre-school. I pulled some kids out of their regular class, read them stories and then did coloring and construction-paper-type activities with them to help their motor skills. There were two main teachers and a few parents that helped out the teachers. One of the teachers, Divina, had been very nice to me. She was only a year older than me. She was from the coastal region of Oaxaca.

I had a presentation in anthropology due. My professor asked me to read articles in Spanish, but I could write the report in English and I could present in whichever language I was comfortable. We had to present twice within the semester. I was trying hard to translate these articles on the indigenous languages and history of Oaxaca. The problem was that so many of these terms were not in my Spanish/English dictionary. Just as I was ready to give up, Erica knocked on my door. Erica was staying in the room across from me. She was spending a week in Oaxaca. She was getting her doctorate in anthropology from NYU and was fluent in Spanish. She asked me if I wanted to hang out with her and some friends that night, and I told her about this difficult article I had to read. She reminded me that she was an anthropology guru and was able to help me with all the questions I had. She helped me for about ten minutes which was enough for me to understand and keep writing my report. She said she would check on me when she got back to see if I had anymore questions. When she got back around midnight, I had a few more questions ready for her.

When I think about all the people that God had placed in my life, if only for a day, a week, or a month, I could see how he chose to take care of me while I was out here by myself. What were the odds that a person like Erica would stay in a room across from me, all the way from New York, the week that I had to make my presentation? I loved how God worked and how He connected people to one another. I know that sometimes figuring out our connections may not always be that easy, and that God can be mysterious at times. But sometimes, He is just so in your face, giving you what you want to show how much He loves you. I felt so blessed seeing the awesomeness of God's work. Erica was a small blessing. In the short time that I was there, God was placing really sincere and good-hearted people in my life. I was grateful for that, because sometimes I am naïve and there are people that could be taking advantage of me because of that. I knew that God did not make things happen just for me, but He used each occurrence for me and my path to show me that He is always in my company, watching over me.

After my second day of fieldwork, Raquel agreed to meet me for lunch at one of the restaurants off the *zocalo*. Because Raquel was in Oaxaca the semester before, she knew of all these great inexpensive restaurants with very friendly waiters. Javier was a young waiter who was always very hospitable. Raquel introduced me to another waiter; his name was Elijah. He had asked me out, but I turned him down, because to be honest, I was not that attracted to him. I told him maybe another day. Today was not good for me. Tonight I was going to go see Neftali at work and go out with him when he got off work.

I went to El Refugio around eleven to see if Marilyn was there. She tended to go there alone. She was there doing her homework since she decided to stay and re-enroll into the Spanish school. Neftali saw me right away and pointed in the section that he was working, but I pointed to the section where Marilyn was sitting. While we were there, these two guys came up to us and started flirting. All the workers were watching to see what we would do, especially Neftali. I do not know about Marilyn, but I found them to be too pretentious. They were telling us of places they could take us and how expensive they were. I told him that I was not interested and that I was leaving in a bit, but he kept insisting. Neftali signaled to me that he was ready to leave, and so I excused myself and walked out with him.

"What were those guys saying to you?" Neftali asked me.

"You know, the usual. 'I was the prettiest girl in the world and doesn't God know an angel is missing from heaven.'" He was laughing at my sarcasm. "They wanted to take us to that restaurant above the theater. And what kind of car they drive. I just said I wasn't interested."

"My friends were making fun of me, saying I wasn't going to have a girlfriend anymore," said Neftali.

"You don't have a girlfriend." I smiled at him as he grabbed my hand, draped his arm around my shoulder, and kissed the side of my face.

"Did you want to go out with them?" he asked.

"No, I don't even know them. I'm sure you weren't worried," I said.

"I knew you were leaving with me." We stopped on the sidewalk to kiss and then I asked him where he was taking me. We went to a pretty popular bar, *Kaos*. We danced a little and had a few drinks, and then we left. He asked me if I was ready to go and did I want to go to our usual spot, the auditorium steps. I said yes and we left.

"I think it's official," Neftali said.

"What?" I asked.

"When I want to leave to New Jersey," he responded.

"When is that?" I asked.

"In March. I gave my two weeks' notice," he informed me.

"To me?" I said, smiling. I knew this was a little hard for him to tell me.

"To the restaurant. The end of February will be my last day. A few of the musicians are leaving that day too, so we have a plan to drink while we're working to make our last day more fun," he explained.

"That's around my birthday!" Once we got to the top we continued our conversation.

"I just want to get outta here," he said.

"Why? It doesn't seem so bad here. I really like it now," I said.

"I just think things will be better out there," he said.

"What things? The things that are going on inside of you? You think moving, running away from all your worries is going to solve all your problems? Maybe it might be a little better, but if your struggles are within, moving isn't going to make them go away. You can't escape your problems, you have to deal with them otherwise they will never go away. If you want to be happy, you have to deal with and confront all those negative emotions inside of you and come to terms with what you have been through in order to get to where you want to be. If you really believe in God, you have to believe that He wants to protect you, and He can, so long as you let Him. God is the most powerful force to have on your side." I grabbed his hands and turned up his wrists. "Imagine if you ever wished you weren't on this earth anymore. From that point on think of all the great experiences and people you would have missed out on if that were to happen. Think about all those great things in your life that have made you really happy. Don't you think God has a lot more happy moments like that just waiting for you? And a lot of really great people that are willing to love you," I told him.

Neftali was quiet the whole time I talked and then I stopped and after a brief silence he said, "That's what I've been needing to hear. I waited a long time to hear something like that. Right now I feel like being alone, but I'm glad you're here with me."

"You can take me home if you want," I said.

"No, I want to be right here with you. It's a nice feeling when you have someone to care about," he said.

I grabbed his face and looked in his eyes and said, "And someone that cares about you."

He Still Loves You

I'd willingly go to the ends of the earth
to help you find God's kingdom.
He has known since before your birth,
the harsh scars your soul would endure.

And He still loves you!

I'd reach out to grab hold of your slipping fingertips,
to take you to the Father's loving arms.
He has felt the shaken weakness of your grip,
lifeless from your fearful emptiness.

But He still loves you!

I'd sacrifice my own comfortable peace,
to lift your soul to the Lord's compassion.
He will cleanse your soul through a harmonic release,
of your demonic corruptions.

Because He still loves you!

I'd listen with an embracing ear
to guide you to the word of the Almighty.
He will speak in a thunderous voice to redirect your fear,
so you will learn to faithfully obey.

Since He still loves you!

I'd spend my days praying the beads in your name,
to demonstrate our faith that He walked on earth.
He will bare your hidden heart of shame,
so you can hold your head high with humility.

For He still loves you!

I'd ask the Creator of heaven and earth to take me to His kingdom today
if He promised today that He would save your soul for eternity.

Because I still love you!

We talked a little more about what he expected New Jersey to be like and I told him what it was like living in the United States. Of course, it would be just another instance like little David. He was a waiter in Mexico; what did he think life was going to be like in a country like the United States with that as his work experience? We sat on the steps overlooking the world. I felt good about everything I said to him. I felt as though it was God working through me, that it was some of what God wanted him to know. I also felt like there were going to be other pretty important people in Neftali's life that were going to help him get closer to God throughout his journey, and as though I had served my purpose and it was time to move on.

THE LORD APPEARED

Then the Lord said, "Go outside and stand on the mountain before the Lord; the Lord will be passing by." A strong and heavy wind was rendering the mountains and crushing rocks before the Lord—but the Lord was not in the wind. After the wind there was an earthquake—but the Lord was not in the earthquake. After the earthquake came a fire—but the Lord was not in the fire. After the fire, there was a tiny whisper sound. When he heard this, Elijah hid his face in his cloak and went and stood at the entrance of the cave.

1 Kings 19:11-13

The next day Marilyn came by and asked me if I wanted to have lunch at La Fogata. Elijah, the waiter, asked me when we could go out, again. I told him I still did not know, because I was always busy. I made plans to hang out with Divina later in the evening. Her boyfriend was taking her out to a club and she had invited me to go. I waited for her in the *zocalo*, and we met her boyfriend at a club called El Snob, in English, "The Snob."

On Saturday Raquel and I had tickets to the theater and had planned to go to the planetarium first. The concert at the theater, we found, was pretty boring, and so we left at intermission. We went to El Refugio. Marilyn was there, and Neftali was working that night. Raquel had brought her camera to take pictures of the different places we were visiting. When we were at the restaurant, it was pretty busy. On Friday and Saturday nights they open the bottom floor and have a bar and a live band for dancing. So that night Neftali was working the bottom floor, but he would come up and visit with us any chance he had. That was when Raquel took our picture. He was pretty excited about that picture and told her that he wanted a copy. He told me that I was someone that he did not want to forget when he left or for the rest of his life. He got off after one that night. It was pretty busy because the next day was Valentine's Day. He walked me home, and we just sat at the park and talked and kissed for a few hours. He said that he wanted to be up early the next day, which was ironic since it was already late.

On Monday Raquel and I went to El Refugio for lunch. Neftali whistled to me from the kitchen. He was not wearing his uniform. He had never come out to talk to me. We had made a date for Wednesday, but Wednesday came and went, and I had not heard from him. I felt a little different this time about him standing me up, because I had already done what God wanted us to do for each other. Marilyn had come over and asked if I wanted to get something to eat. I told her that I did, but that I wanted to go to La Fogata. I told her what had happened with Neftali, and she told me that he had not been at work since Sunday. I had decided to write off that relationship. I did not want to dwell over what could have happened to him and how could he have done this to me. I figured he was going through a more difficult time than I was. So when I was at La Fogata I agreed to go out with Elijah. The main reason why I wanted to go out with him was because he was nice and he seemed eager, which is flattering. Besides, I was there to have fun, to get to see as much of Oaxaca as I could. It made sense to share that with the people that were natives of the state. After Marilyn and I ate, we went to church. She was not Catholic, but I was, and it was Ash Wednesday.

The next day I met Raquel for lunch at La Fogata. Elijah was there. He was asking me what kind of activities I liked to do. I told him that whatever he had in mind was fine. Javier, the other waiter, was making fun of Elijah for being able to "score a date with me." He got very shy and embarrassed. He seemed intimidated by me. Even when he was asking me out, it was not him that was asking. It was Raquel telling me that he was interested in me and if I would give him a chance. He was just standing there smiling. I wondered what he would be like without Raquel. When I got home I checked my e-mail. I had a message from Solomon. He was telling me that the literary and art annual was published by the university and he grabbed a few copies for me. He submitted art work, and I submitted a story that I wrote about my brother, Angel.

It was Friday morning when Martha knocked on my door and told me that Neftali was downstairs and he wanted to see me. I told her to tell him he could come upstairs to the room. I looked at the time and it was nine in the morning. "I got you outta bed, huh?" Neftali asked.

"You woke me up, but I'm staying in bed," I said.

He sat on the bed next to me. He hugged me and ran his hand over my hair and stared at me. "I came by Wednesday and Thursday, but no one was here."

"What's going on?" I asked.

"I got into it with the manager at work, so I just quit. When you saw me Monday, I was just there getting my last wages. I had enough, you know?" he said.

"So what are you going to do?" I asked.

"Well, I'm just gonna get ready to go out to my cousin's," he said.

"In New Jersey?"

"Yeah," he responded.

"Weren't you supposed to leave this month? In a week or something, right?" I was giving him a hard time.

"Yeah, I was supposed to, but my cousin said to wait until April," he said.

"Oh, so now you're going to leave in April, and when April comes, May, and then June, until you turn around and its September and you're still here," I said.

"What are you trying to say?" asked Neftali.

"Nothing," I responded.

"Did Raquel develop those pictures yet?" he asked.

"I don't think so," I said.

It was getting late and I had class at eleven and still had to shower and do all my morning rituals.

Neftali said that he liked being the one who woke me up and that he would come over tomorrow morning to do it again. So Saturday morning he arrived at nine thirty. He just hung out with me until noon and told me that he decided that if he did not leave in April, he was going to go back and live with his mother. He thought that they had to work through some of their issues. She was living in Cancun now, and that was also where his father was. I touched his heart and smiled at him. I said a little prayer for him in my mind, hoping that he would find whatever it was that he was looking for in order to be at peace with himself, God, and those that had caused him distress.

After he left I did homework and worked on my next article. I was writing about the Children's Hospital in Oaxaca. The hospital needed lots of monetary donations and volunteers, because they charged people whatever they were willing to pay. I was intrigued by that concept, because when my grandfather was a healer, he would know how to massage and help fix people when they had hurt limbs. He had owned a ranch of cows, and he would have to heal the bones and limbs of the cows when they were injured. He learned that the skeleton of an animal was not that different from a human skeleton. He never charged people anything they could not afford. He also accepted any type of pay besides monetary, like food, animals, clothing, anything. I spent a whole summer with him once and had learned just how amazing he was. But that is for another story. I was very close to my grandfather, and he was someone that I admired immensely, so I admired the hospital, the way they chose to help people. It meant a lot to me to be able to help them.

Elijah and I had agreed to meet at the Cathedral in the *zocalo* at six. He showed up about ten minutes late and very upset. He had told me that another restaurant asked him to work the night shift, and if he would have said no he would have gotten in trouble. He was disappointed, because he did not want me to be upset and decide not to go out with him anymore. I told him I understood and that it was fine; I would not hold it against him. He was working at a little restaurant near El Regufio and asked if we could meet after he got off work. He only had to work a few hours and would be off by eleven. We just hung out and talked for a bit, and then I walked with him to his work. I told him I would meet him back here around eleven. I went to El Refugio, because I figured Marilyn would be there. We went to the bottom floor to dance and have a few drinks, and I left at eleven to go meet Elijah.

He took me to an underground club. It was like the movie *Dirty Dancing*, because I had recognized waiters and bartenders from different bars and restaurants. The club was called Tattoo. No "the" or "*El*" or anything, just Tattoo. It was big and had lots of booths and tables along the edges. The dance floor was huge and packed with people. You could only see their faces and different body parts moving quickly, but the change of the colored lights made them look as though they were moving even faster. He brought me a beer, and I drank it slowly. I did not want to dance in the sea of all those people. We did not talk much, because it was too loud for us to have a conversation. We were only there for about two hours, and then he walked me home.

I have to admit that I was the worst, most boring, first date ever. I did not even finish my beer. I did not want to dance, and we were at a club. The whole way we walked home I only let him hold my hand. I do not know why I felt so cautious. I cannot help but feel scared when I begin to date someone new. Even if I do not know what will happen or can happen. I fear getting attached and then not having that person that I got used to in my life anymore. In the back of my mind I was hoping that he would not have fun and would not like me. But when we got to my door he kissed me on the cheek, said he had fun and asked me when we could see each other again.

The next week I ran into Neftali. I was walking home from class, and he was out running errands. He asked me if I had no where to be, could I accompany him. So I did. Then he walked me home and came in for a while. He was only here for about an hour. He seemed so different from when we first met. He seemed lost, like he was unsure as to what he wanted out of life and for his future. I cared about him, about what would happen to him, but I knew that I did not have romantic feelings for him. Later that evening I met Elijah at the cathedral again. We walked around the *zocalo* and he bought me a *paleta de limón*. He was so curious about everything. He talked a lot and told me a lot about himself. Every time he asked me an odd question about myself, he listened to me so attentively with a great big smile and two adorable dimples in his cheeks. His big brown eyes were large with curiosity and amazement at my responses. I felt safe with him. He was naïve like me, and that made me trust him.

The next day Neftali came over around four in the evening. We walked to the auditorium stairs and talked. He seemed nervous and melancholy. His depression was something I did not know how to handle. He did not even seem like he liked me as much as he had. He was reminding me of Luke more and more, where I was a new kind of high in the beginning, but after awhile his real issues would just resume. He walked me home and stayed for awhile and then left around seven. He said that he would try to stop by soon but he had not. He disappeared, like the other times, but this time he had not made any efforts to resurface.

I went to the pre-school in the morning and then I went to La Fogata for lunch to see Elijah. I was studying for my test, so I spent a couple of hours there. He would come around to check on me and bring me chocolate cake and cookies, sweet things that I did not order, and before I left, he would not bring me the bill. We had agreed to meet at the cyber café when I got out of class and he was off work. We had checked our e-mails, and he was showing me websites he liked.

I got an e-mail from Solomon, but I did not want to read it in front of Elijah. So when I got home I checked my e-mail again. Solomon was telling me all about his mid-terms and what had been going on at school with our mutual friends. He asked me what I planned on doing for my birthday. It was Sunday, but I wanted to celebrate it on Saturday at a salsa place called La Candela. I wanted to invite the few close friends that I had made. What I had been unsure about was whether or not I should ask Elijah to be my date since we had barely started dating.

Friday, Elijah and I met in the park. I was sitting on a bench and he was walking over to me, with a huge smile on his face. I could not help but laugh. He kissed me on the cheek and began to ask so many questions as he normally did. "Did you wait long?" I shook my head no. "How was your day? You didn't have any classes? Did you hang out with Raquel and Marilyn?"

"My day was good. No, I didn't have any classes so, yes, I did hang out with Raquel and Marilyn," I responded, smiling.

"Let's sit down for a minute; I feel tired," suggested Elijah. We sat on the bench and he put his head on my shoulder while I stroked his cheek. "I had a long day at work. I got in an argument with a co-worker and the boss yelled at me, because he said I should know better. He only yelled at me because he likes me a lot and looks out for me and he did not want me to get into trouble with the owner. But it wasn't even my fault. He gave the other guy a warning, and documented it but barely said anything to him."

"He wasn't saying it was your fault. He just expected better from you. Isn't that good, that someone thinks that highly of you?" I said.

"Yeah, but the other guy should have gotten yelled at, too," he said.

"He did get a written warning, and you only got a verbal warning. Isn't a written warning worse? That means it can lead to getting fired," I said.

"Yeah, I guess you're right." Elijah got a smile back on his face and kissed me in appreciation on the cheek. His problems were a lot easier to solve than Neftali's. We had not had our first kiss yet, and he was so shy and sweet I did not know if we ever would. He seemed to try so hard not to do anything to offend me.

"Are you rested now? Can we walk around?" I asked.

"Yeah, I feel better now. You made me feel better." We got up and walked around the *zocalo*. I told him how I felt about walking on the inside of the man as a sexist action. In which case, he did not care that I wanted to walk on the outside to spite the culture. He thought it was cute and did not feel his masculinity threatened at all.

"Did you know that Sunday is my birthday? My friends and I are meeting at La Candela tomorrow night. Will you come?" I asked Elijah.

"Isn't that place kinda fancy?" he replied.

"I don't really know. I have never been there but I have heard great things about it and I really wanna go. Martha, the lady that I rent from, plays in a band there," I said.

"What do they play?" He asked.

"Salsa," I said.

"Salsa! I don't know how to dance that," he said.

"But it's my birthday, and this is what I want. I really want you there with me," I said.

"All right. I'm gonna go, but I want to ask you something."

"What?" I asked.

"I want to know if you want to be my girlfriend?" Based on his question, I could tell that he was naïve and sweet, shy and sincere. "I really like you and I want us to spend time together, just you and me," he said eagerly.

"I like you, too, and I would really like to continue to get to know you, but, as far as a committed relationship is concerned, I don't think that's a good idea," I said.

"Why not?" he asked.

"What's the point? I am only going to be here for a few months. I am not saying that I want to keep dating other people. I don't mind dating only you, but to be in a commitment feels like too much pressure. I think we have fun, and I just want to take it slow; I don't want a serious relationship," I responded.

"So no?" he confirmed.

"Elijah, I like you a lot, and I want to keep dating you. I want you to be my date for my birthday celebration. Isn't that enough to prove how much I like you?" I asked.

"I understand," he said, defeated.

He walked me home at the end of the night and told me he would see me on Saturday. He gave me a kiss on the cheek. I decided to egg him on for a little more. "Don't you want to kiss me?" I asked him.

"Yeah, but I don't know if you'll get upset," Elijah said, sheepishly.

"Well, how are you going to know if you don't try?" I said.

"I would just rather ask you," he said.

"When did you have in mind to ask me?" I said.

"Can I ask you now?" he said.

"Can you ask me now if you can kiss me? Yeah, go ahead," I said, smiling.

"Can I kiss you?"

"No." And I kissed him on the cheek. "You can kiss me tomorrow." He just smiled.

Saturday after laundry and some homework, I thought about Elijah's question. I know it sounds funny, but I really wanted to be that sweet, shy, sincere naïve guy's girlfriend; I liked Elijah's positive and optimistic attitude. I knew that I was not that attracted to him, but I thought so much of him, because that was how he made me feel inside.

I had rested a while and then got all pretty for my birthday celebration. Around eight, Divi called me and said that she was on her way. About ten minutes later, Marilyn came over. She was excited, because this new guy she was seeing said that he would meet her there, too. She had given me roses, which I appreciated very much. Once Divi got there, we took a taxi to the salsa club. Martha was there, because she was going to be playing with the band. She told our waiter to take great care of me, because I was special to her and it was my birthday. By the end of the night, the only other people that showed up were Elijah and one of his friends. I had invited Raquel as well, but she did not come. Marilyn was upset, because the man she invited did not show up, either. Divi and Marilyn had danced with a few men, but Elijah did not want to dance. I was upset about that. I told him that was the whole point of coming here. I asked him if it would bother him if I danced with someone else. He said yes.

So I did not. It seemed as though everyone felt uncomfortable or out of place with these "kind" of people. Even Divi said that the people were very rude and stuck up. We had something to eat, and Marilyn was the first one to leave around eleven. The rest of us left around midnight. We had walked Divi to the bus and Elijah, his friend, and I went to Tattoo, the club we went to last time. The kind of music they played there was Spanish/English rock and pop, and the later it got, the more they played house and techno music. It was supposed to enhance the mood of people being hopped up on alcohol and drugs by then. It was funny, the irony of being in one place that was elegant and fancy and then going to a place that seemed like a giant barn with a disco ball. Elijah felt a lot more comfortable; he started dancing and having a drink himself. After he got out some of his energy on the dance floor, he and I grabbed a table to sit.

"Leizel, do you want to leave?" Elijah asked me.

"No, I am fine. If you still want to dance, we can dance," I said.

"No, I am good. I had enough. Can we just go outside and sit and walk in the *zocalo*?" he said.

"You want to?" I asked.

"Yes." We left the club and walked around the town. It was such a nice, cool night.

"What happened to your friend?" I asked Elijah.

"He left already. I told him I was going to have to walk you home and that he should just leave whenever he wanted," he replied.

"So I take it that you did not enjoy yourself at the place I picked?" I asked.

"It isn't that, I just felt uncomfortable. That was where all the rich people go," he said.

"Why would you say that? How do you even notice something like that?" I asked.

"You don't notice, because you are more like them than me," he said.

"What is that supposed to mean?"

"It means that you and I are different. We're different social classes. You're in college and your parents help you," he said.

"That makes me rich?" I tried to understand.

"I don't have the luxury of going to college or have my parents help me with whatever I need. My dad left my mom several years ago. He left all of us, my two sisters and my brother. I am the oldest boy, and I have to work. I have to take care of my family now. Like that day I couldn't say no to work, I needed that money. I can't spend money to take you to places like tonight. I have to send my brother and sisters to school and help my mom. She has to work and be on her feet all day. And she has problems and can barely be on her feet. She needs surgery soon," he explained.

"Okay, so maybe we are from different social classes. So what?" I said.

"You might not like that," Elijah said.

"I'm not the one who noticed. I'm not the one complaining about it right now."

"Yeah, but if I don't say something you'll eventually notice it for yourself," he suggested.

"Look, I am the child of two very hard-working parents. They have made a lot of sacrifices to be able to let me take advantage of opportunities like this one; it doesn't mean that I have it easy. So if you have a problem with that then just tell me now, and we can make this our last date," I said defensively.

"I don't want this to be our last date," he assured me.

"Then what is your point? Are you saying you don't want to go out with me anymore, when just the other day you were trying to convince me to be your girlfriend?" I asked.

"No, I really like you and I want to be with you. I just want you to know that sometimes I am not going to be able to take you to places like tonight and that I might have other responsibilities because of my family."

"So why didn't you just say that in the beginning?" I asked.

"I want to be honest with you about who I am."

"And I like who you are and I don't care about social class, or money or material things." With that said, he grabbed my face and kissed me. We had our first kiss. I know I usually brag about great first kisses, but I could tell he was not that experienced. That did not matter to me. I felt like I was with someone more on my emotional level.

The next day was my birthday. I had planned to leave for Mass at one. I usually went to Santo Domingo, because now where I lived, it was not out of my way, and it was still the prettiest church closest to me. And after four when Elijah got off work, I met him at the cathedral and we just hung out at the *zocalo,* talked and practiced our kissing. He was always so happy and laughing. I had a good time with him.

As time went on, Elijah and I saw each other every day. Because I was working through the lending library, I was also spending a lot of time reading. I had to report there every now and then, and so I would see books and want to read them. Besides that, Martha would recommend books to me. Aside from being a great musician, she had a psychology degree and recommended some self-help books like, *A Woman's Worth* by Marrianne Williamson. I had read a book by Junot Diaz, *Drown.* I found it culturally inspiring. After that I started to read Frida Kahlo's autobiography. I have always admired her. I read her biography once before in high school and did a report on it. I have always wanted to be a writer. Journalism was a great outlet, but I felt as though there was little room for creativity.

Elijah had gotten so used to me that he took my time for granted. He brought me a late birthday gift. It was an imitation Winnie the Pooh stuffed bear. He was still convincing me to be his girlfriend. He said that I was playing with his emotions. I knew it was actually more to protect my emotions. Eventually I gave in to his request. I wrote him a note. I always wrote him letters. It was the best way I knew how to communicate my feelings. He loved getting letters from me. In the letter I told him that if being "his girlfriend" was going to make him feel more secure, than fine. He became a big part of my life. I saw him two or three times a day. We would meet before class, after class, before work, after work, and spend all our days off together visiting friends. We became that couple people hated, because we were inseparably cute. The most annoying thing about us was how we would sing love songs with each other. He would sing one line first and then I would sing the next, then him, then me, and so on. Our favorite songs to sing together were *Como Te Voya Olvidar* by Angeles Azules and *Nunca Te Olvidaré*, by Enrique Iglesias, songs that encompassed how we would never forget who we were for each other. But it was hard sometimes being in a relationship, because he had all these expectations of me, and I was not always good at meeting them. I was not used to being considerate of someone else all the time.

One day he came over after work but said that he could not stay long, because he had not spent time with his friends lately, and I agreed. About twenty minutes later, Marilyn showed up asking me to go out to dinner, and so, assuming he wanted to leave early, I went with her. This upset him. The next day, we were at Raquel's place. She was just making small talk that led Elijah and me into a big disagreement. "What are you guys doing tomorrow?" Raquel asked us.

I chimed in right away. "Oh, I have to go to the inauguration at the pre-school I volunteer at. They're also doing the spring prince and princess election and ceremony and having a little party afterwards. It should be a fun experience," I said.

"When were you going to tell me this?" he asked with shock.

"I'm telling you now. It isn't that big of a deal. I was invited since I have been volunteering these several months," I told him.

"What if I had plans for us?" Elijah asked.

"Well, when were you gonna tell me that?" I asked.

He looked around, and we took the rest of the conversation outside. "Why didn't you tell me? I could have gone with you."

"I don't want you to come with me. This a like a work/school thing. You have your work schedule, and I have mine. My work isn't as important as your work?" I asked.

"No, but you don't include me in your life. I wanted to go spend time with you after work," he said.

"So it's okay for you to just assume I'm free and make plans without consulting me, but not okay for me to make my own plans without consulting you? You never asked me if you could come over or what I was doing. How can you say I don't include you in my life? We're always together," I informed him.

"It's just like yesterday, you went out with Marilyn and didn't even invite me," he said.

"You said you were gonna leave early to be with your friends. You didn't invite me to go hang out with your friends, and I didn't care. I want to give you your space, because I know I need my own space, too, sometimes," I said.

"Well, it would have been nice if you had asked me anyway. And so what? I'm not gonna see you tomorrow?" he said.

"I'll be home by six or seven. Sorry to inconvenience you. God forbid I have a life of my own. I told you I wasn't going to be a good girlfriend. And now you're putting all this pressure on me, and I don't even understand how you can be upset, because you are doing the same thing," I said.

That is how I felt. God had sent me far away from my family to learn how to be independent and here was Elijah, trying to take away my independence. Honestly, it just gave me one more reason why I knew being in a relationship was not what God wanted for me now, and for a while. The main reason I told him that it might not be a good reason to be together was that eventually I had to leave, and that was going to be hard, but he did not care. We went on with our relationship, spending most of our free time together for several months more. I still did the things that I wanted to do, like my volunteer work for the newspaper. After having written the article on the hospital, I received an invitation to take a personal tour of it. It was an exciting recognition, but it was sad to see the many children in the hospital for different purposes. It was rewarding knowing I had helped them, knowing that I was serving God.

Solomon was e-mailing me regularly until I told him about Elijah. In his last e-mail he gave me the third degree and then he just stopped e-mailing me after that. He wrote about school and money problems, and how much he missed me. He said it was stupid for me to be in a relationship with someone this soon, and how serious could it even be when I am going to be home soon. I did not know how to respond to the e-mail. Was he jealous, angry, just being overprotective, or happy for me? I just ignored it. I figured I would be going home in a few weeks anyway, and would deal with it then.

Martha, my host, was telling me how much she had seen me change and blossom into a beautiful young woman. She called me a woman. By age, technically I was, but I had never felt like I was yet. She said even my thought process had seemed more mature, and that at times she felt like she had a little sister, but when I would offer her advice, my perspective was so mature that she felt like the little sister. I see in her someone that God sent me to find. She helped me cope with so many issues. Her honesty and sincerity and genuine concern and care also made me see that I did have the capacity to be loved and to love, just in a different way than I had always been expecting. She cared for me like a mother, when not too long ago I was a stranger. I know she was one of the only few people that I let inside my heart. I showed her how hypersensitive I could be, and even how afraid I could be. My relationship with Elijah made me see what I had to do if I wanted to be in a serious relationship and that presently I was still not emotionally ready. What was so nice about this relationship was that he allowed me to be true to God. I never had to fight temptation with him.

Until We Meet Again

Here I am in a foreign place,
but I know it's not for long.
Instantly you became a familiar face,
but strangely it seemed wrong.
Wrong, because if I fall in love,
and turn around and leave,
then all the dreams that we thought of
one day we'll never achieve.
When the time comes to return to you,
will my place already be taken?
Or will your thoughts of me accrue
to a point where I will never be forsaken?
I'll kiss you good-bye and be on my way
and pray this won't be the end.
I'll be looking forward to the day
until we meet again.

The last week or two were the hardest, because slowly Elijah would pull away. We ended our relationship as emotionally painless as possible. I wrote him a final letter and gave him two folders my sister had sent from my university with the school emblem on them. He gave me a stuffed heart that said, "I love you." We kept in touch through e-mail. The day I left, he called and said, "You know what? I miss you." It gave me time to reflect on those past several months, understanding why God brought me all the way over there. But looking back, I know I had grown into a woman. I learned to be independent. I learned to find God and know that being alone does not mean you have to be lonely, especially when you are with God. I knew that this experience was preparing me for the bigger picture of God's plan. I was no longer lost and no longer waiting. Through his children and through my faith and actions, the Lord appeared to me.

THE WISE CHOICE

When all Israel heard the judgment the king had given, they were in awe of him, because they saw that the king had in him the wisdom of God for giving judgment….God gave Solomon wisdom and exceptional understanding and knowledge, as vast as the sand on the seashore. Solomon surpassed all…in wisdom. He was wiser than all other men.

1 Kings 3:38, 5:9-11

It was on this plane ride home when I had the vision from God telling me that I already met the person whom I would love and serve in my life. I began to pay close attention to all with whom I would reunite. As I had said previously, I was not sure if this thought would be something that I needed to heed from God, or if it was all in my imagination.

After a couple of days of reacquainting myself with my family, I began to contact my friends. Judith was the first person I called.

"How does it feel to be back?" Judith asked.

"It feels good," I said.

"Yeah, was it hard to come back?" she asked.

"A little, I guess. But it feels good; I'm happy to be back," I replied.

"Have you talked to anyone else?"

"No, not yet." I told her how Elijah and I spent our last few days. Honestly, the next person I wanted to talk to was Solomon. We had not communicated through e-mail after I had told him about Elijah, and I wondered if he would speak to me or how he would respond to me. I called him and left him a message. He called me right back and told me that he was down the street at a friend's house.

"So you're finally back, huh?" Solomon asked.

"Yeah, what are you doing?" I asked.

"I'm at Jose's, down the street. I figured I'd stop by if that was cool," he said.

"That'd be great." I said. When he arrived, right away he gave me a hug.

"Wow, you look great!" Solomon exclaimed.

"Thanks, so do you." His hair was short again, he had recently cut it. "What happened to your Jesus hair?" I asked.

"Well, I cut it off for the summer. So how was it?" he asked.

"It was great. I had a lot of fun, and I met someone that I didn't expect to meet," I said.

"That guy you wrote me about?" I sensed some sarcasm in his voice.

"No, someone better."

"Who?" he asked.

"God. I met God through so many people," I responded.

He asked me a lot of questions about the trip and the people I met. I had a few pictures that I shared with him to show him the faces that went with the all the names, and the amazing views I took in of beaches, mountains, and towns. He sat with me for a couple of hours. After all, it was a nice breezy May evening. Just before he was getting ready to leave, he leaned over and gave me another hug. "I'm glad you're back. I really did miss hanging out with you," he said.

"Wait, before you go, I want to give you something I got you from Mexico." I gave him two gifts. The first was a necklace, black cord with a silver and wooden cross. "I hope you like it. If you don't like it, you don't have to take it."

"No, I like it. I'll wear it, thank you." The next thing I gave him was a medium-size statue of the Mayan's belief of the three stages of life. Each facial expression emerged from the last, birth, adulthood, and death. I explained the meaning of it. Since Solomon was into art, I thought it was the perfect gift for him. Like me, he was very much into the history and culture of South American countries. He was half Peruvian, but I had not found much on Inca culture. I had explained its cultural meaning and background to him, and he listened so intently to my eyes as I spoke to him with the passion of the gift's significance. "Where did you get it?" Solomon asked.

"From a gift shop at one of the ruins we visited," I said.

"How did you know all that other stuff?" he asked.

"Well, one of the tour guides told me a little bit, and then I asked my anthropology professor about it. He's very knowledgeable," I responded.

"Well, thanks. This is really cool, and I really appreciate what you did to learn about it," he said.

"I'm glad you like it," I said, smiling.

"I'll call you later and let you know what's going on. Someone is having a birthday party this weekend," he said, as he walked to his car.

"Sounds good. Drive safely."

At the end of the night, I said my prayers. A tear rolled down my cheek remembering Elijah and all the wonderful memories we left behind. I wondered if I would ever see him again and if he was thinking about me, and then I drifted off to sleep.

The weekend came and Solomon offered to pick me up and take me with him to the party to celebrate the birthday of one of our friends from Saint Ambrose. My old roommate, Lily, and all our mutual friends from school would be there, and I was excited to see them. I had gotten special little gifts for each of them as I did for Solomon. When he arrived for me, I noticed that he was wearing the necklace I had given him, and that made me happy. Solomon and I played slug bug on the way there; I won, twelve to seven. Even though I had fun at the party, the highlight was spending time with Solomon. The summertime was usually mellow. I spent a lot of time with my family and friends, going for runs and sleeping. I thought about Elijah a lot as well, and every day I would check my e-mail in hopes that I would hear from him. It was actually about two weeks after I left when he finally sent me an e-mail. It read, "Hi!"

Hi! I expected something of substance or thought. I thought maybe he was just learning how to use e-mail and it was just a practice e-mail or something.

A few days after that, I had a dream about Solomon. For the first time he was taking a trip to Peru to meet his family, and he had left a few days ago. In the dream he had these piercing blue eyes and this glowing white pale skin, which is what he looked like, but he appeared more vibrant and heavenly. He was holding me, and I was crying.

I had told Judith about my dream and how I had this angelic image of Solomon.

"That happens sometimes, when you admire someone so much, you tend to have this distorted image of their appearance. They seem more perfect than they really are," Judith said.

"Yeah, and there isn't much more perfection than one of God's angels," I said.

"It's like, because you like him for so many reasons, you're taking the beauty that you see within him and then it embellishes the perfection of the reflection on the outside," she explained.

"Maybe God was trying to tell me something about him," I said.

"Maybe you just miss him since he's on vacation. When does he get back?" she asked.

"I don't know. I guess he was going to be gone for a couple of weeks," I said.

I had not received another e-mail from Elijah until two weeks later. It was a little longer than before, but not much. He had written the reason for which he had not written. Basically, he was so busy working, but he had so much to tell me. Yet he was in a hurry to get to work now and therefore he would try to write more at a later time. I did not know how to feel about Elijah. Was there a future for us? Was it worth trying to maintain a friendship with him if I was never going to see him again? Would maintaining a friendship with him prevent me from exploring other relationships? But the hope within me that is based on God's faith deep down inside makes me believe in people.

Solomon called me when he returned from Peru. He spent three hours telling me all about what he did, his family, and what Peru was like. He was so excited to finally be able to experience Peru. My sister and I were going to have a small gathering of about ten people. We invited a few close friends. Solomon had brought a couple of bottles of Pisco, which is a Peruvian liquor extracted from grapes. At the end of the night, Solomon was not in a condition to drive home. He asked me to recommend him some good books from Latin American authors. He had associated me with literature as I had associated him with art. We talked about Spanish rock music we both liked and made plans to go to a few concerts. There was a sense of comfort, a knowledge of a line that neither one of us would ever cross that was established between two good friends, the kind of line that if crossed, you could never go back to what you had. When he fell asleep on my couch, I kissed him on the cheek. I stared at him for a while, trying to see the brilliant angel that had been in my dream. I placed a blanket over him and then went to my own bed. I wondered if I would ever have the courage to tell him how much I admired him.

Little by little I received more e-mails from Elijah. He had reflected a lot on our relationship since I had been gone, which was obvious in his e-mails. He apologized for having been selfish with me and not always being patient with me. He told me how supportive and sweet I had always been with him regardless of his impatience and errors. It was clear that we had missed each other very much, and secretly, I was planning a trip back to Oaxaca before the end of the summer. Elijah had indicated that I should visit again in August because of the *Guelaguetza* in July. It brought in too many tourists, which brought a lot of work for him. And that was what I had done. I had planned to go back and visit the second week of August.

In the meantime, Solomon and I were spending lots of time together, at least more time than friends would normally spend. We had gone to two concerts, however nothing beyond that would ever happen. I do not know if that was what I expected. Solomon asked me if I wanted to go to a bookstore and recommend some books to buy. He knew that bookstores were my weakness. The only Peruvian writer we found was *The Feast of the Goat* by Mario Vargas Llosa. Then we found books by basic Latin American authors such as Gabriel Garcia Marquez, Pablo Nerudo, and Juan Rulfo, who was born in Sayula. I made him get *Pedro Paramo*. He liked all that magic realism—macabre genre.

"Thanks for coming with me and suggesting these books to me," said Solomon.

"No problem," I said.

"I got a whole bunch of music out there too, for the show, you know?" he said.

"Oh, really, that's cool. I decided to go back to Mexico at the end of the summer. Is there anything you want me to look for? I asked him.

"You are? Why? Because of that guy?" he asked, disappointed.

"No. To see my family." I did not want him to know that I was going back to see that guy. Not because I thought he would be upset, but I did not want him to judge me for going all the way back there for some guy. Why did he care, anyway?

The time had come to see what I had left behind in Oaxaca. I had planned a week in Oaxaca, and from the beginning it felt like I had never left. I had seen Raquel again. She had dropped out of Saint Ambrose and decided to live a life in Oaxaca. She was happier there than Chicago. I stayed with Martha again. I did see Elijah a few times in the week that I had visited. Initially he asked me to go to the restaurant to see him, but someone's job is not the ideal setting for a reunion. He had agreed to come visit me in my old place, my old room, when he got off work. I let him in, and he kissed me and kissed me again. In the week that I was there, I only saw him three times. He certainly communicated the message I needed to hear effectively. I was no longer a priority; perhaps he did not believe that there was a possibility that one day we would be a part of each other's future.

The last and third night that we spent together was not planned. I asked him if we could spend my last day together, and he said that after he got out of work he was going to go out with his friends. All there was for me to do was understand. That Saturday morning I woke up, showered, and made myself presentable to the world. Deep in my heart I was sad, because I had come so far for an answer, and I had received it. It broke my heart, but I knew that if he was not in God's plan for me anymore, then all I could do was cherish what we had. I went to say good-bye to my other friends, spending a little time with each of them. I went to the cyber café and got home around seven in the evening. Elijah, surprisingly, came over an hour later.

"I'm sorry I wasn't around for you like you wanted. I just couldn't do this again. You're here, and you're gonna leave again. And it's gonna hurt again." He looked around the room. "This is where all our memories are. I came here one day; I showed some lady who was looking for a place to stay."

"I know, Martha told me." I let him talk; it seemed as though he had much more to say.

"I know I acted stupid, but I really do love you." He was looking directly into my eyes with his hand on my cheek. "You're beautiful, intelligent and sweet…but I just don't know how…"

And I guess he did not know how to finish the statement. He hugged me tight and said, "I'm gonna stay with you the whole night, like I should have done the last time. I'm glad I have another chance to make things right." That night was the way I wanted to remember our relationship. We went for a walk around town and then talked for the rest of the night, and shared a few intimate kisses. He continued to respect the boundaries. Eventually we fell asleep. The next morning we woke up together and his mind was back in his Oaxacan realm.

"I have to leave right away," Elijah said.

"Why? Don't you want to go with me to the bus station?" I asked.

"I can't watch you get ready to leave, much less see you leave. But I want you to know I do appreciate how good you have always been to me, and how much you are willing to do for me. You were good to me, maybe too good." I walked him to the door. "Try to write me a lot; don't forget about me." He kissed me softly on the lips, and then again, so I hugged him tight, and then he pulled me back, and we looked at each other in our eyes, and he kissed me again, softly. "Hopefully you'll come back soon," he said. He kissed me softly one last time, to last me until our next encounter; he turned around and walked out of my life, not knowing what would ever become of us again.

The first day of school in August was a gloomy, rainy day, and that was how I had felt emotionally. I had been avoiding Solomon and the confusion of my feelings. It seemed that I had just not wanted to let anyone else in my heart. Elijah meant so much to me. I cared for Solomon, too, but it seemed like God was not going to let me have anyone, at least not right now. I saw Solomon in school, and he had stopped me to give me a hug. "What's going on? How come you haven't called back since you got back from Mexico? How was it?" Solomon asked.

"It was fun." I said.

"Did you see that guy?" he asked.

"I told you I was seeing my family," I said.

"Lily said you saw that guy," he informed me.

"Well, I decided to go for a few days," I confessed.

"What did you do?" he asked, curiously.

"What do you mean, what did I do? Nothing," I said.

"Oh well, I wanna hang out this weekend. Wanna do something?"

"I don't know. I guess it depends on how much homework I have this week," I said.

"It's the first week; no one's gonna give homework. Come on, walk to the computer lab with me," he said. My desire at the computer lab was strictly to see if Elijah had e-mailed me. It had been a couple of weeks since I had been back and had not checked my e-mail to avoid disappointment in case he had not written. Fortunately, Elijah had written me, and I opened his e-mail. He had said that although he was so grateful for spending Saturday night, the last night, with me, he wished he had not been so stubborn the whole week. He regretted not spending more time with me. He missed me so much.

In early October I had called Elijah because of an earthquake in Oaxaca. It hit a magnitude of 7.5, and I was extremely concerned for Elijah and his family's well-being. I called him at work. He had already stressed that we were different when it came to social class. In which case, he did not own a house phone. He said that the sound of my voice made him believe I was still there, speaking from the phone on which he used to call me in Oaxaca. He also said that he and his family were fine. Later he sent me an e-mail expressing his disbelief for calling him out of sheer concern. He had described his fear of the destruction of the earthquake, of the crumbling buildings and shattering glass. The lights had gone out at the restaurant, and everyone scrambled to the phones without paying their bills, leaving the restaurant lifeless.

A few weeks after that, in late October, was Elijah's birthday, and he had asked me to send him more folders with my school emblem etched on them. He liked using them for his own school, and said they reminded him of me, so I sent him a little care package. He wrote a little in English. He always enjoyed practicing his English with me. When he received the folders, he wrote me the longest e-mail he had ever written. He showed off the folders and told people that "his girlfriend" had given them to him. I drew his name in fancy block letters and shaded them on his birthday card, and he had asked me to teach him how to do that the next time we were together. He wrote of business ventures he was planning and often asked me when I thought I would return to see him again. He created illusions of coming to the United States to start a new life with me. I wondered if there would ever be an opportunity, to teach him how to draw the letters.

By mid-November Solomon and I had not been spending as much time together. Ironically he was acting weird about me liking some guy that I no longer even got to see, when he was the one for which I had secret feelings. Maybe he sensed them all along, my feelings for him. One day he came to see me in the writing lab. "It's slow on Fridays, isn't it?" he noticed.

"Yeah, but we still have to stay open," I responded. "What's up?"

"I'm having a party at my house. It's one of my cousin's birthdays, and a lot of friends from where I live are going to be there. Let's hang out. It's been a while. I know I was acting weird, but it's cool. Maybe I was just a little jealous, because I was going through a dry spell, and you were all into some guy and…well, we just didn't hang out as much. But I met this girl last weekend. She's one of my cousin's friends, so she'll be at the party," Solomon admitted.

"Then why do you want me there?" I asked.

"Because you're my friend…and we always have a lot of fun together. So you can have fun, too," he responded.

"Okay, I'll come," I agreed.

"You want me to pick you up?" he asked.

"No, I'll drive myself." I thought it best, in case I could not handle what I saw and decided to leave early. What was the irony here? Was he jealous that I was seeing someone else, and now I am not and now he is over me? Does this mean that I had a chance? Should I have told him how I felt?

"Just come over whenever you want. I don't care if it's early," he said.

"Well, do you need help with anything; do you want me to pick anything up?" I offered.

"Umm…I don't really know. I'll let you know if I do."

Even though I still had feelings for Elijah and I still kept in contact with him, it was not like I was getting to spend time with him.

I showed up late to the party. It was already after nine. I knew Solomon probably expected me to be there a lot earlier, but I lacked the desire to be there at all. Solomon saw me walk in and immediately walked over to me. He introduced me to a lot of friends and some of his cousins. His guests that were local had gone to high school with him, and his cousins and their friends came from different sides of Chicago. His radio show partner, Eric, paid me an extra amount of attention. I met Cherri, his new friend. Solomon had a type, and she fit it, pale skin, dark long black hair and black lacy clothes. All of his chivalry was being used on some other girl. When Eric offered me a beer, I accepted. When he offered me a shot, I accepted. I knew this was not the way to deal with confused emotions, but for the time being I was at a party and I wanted to have fun and allow myself to be distracted from Solomon. Eric had an agenda of his own; he would bring me drinks, and we would dance. Solomon was checking on me from time to time. He would ask me if I was feeling well, make sure I did not over do it, and once I did, he would put a stop to it.

"Are you having fun, Leizel?" Solomon asked.

"Yeah, your boy Eric is looking out for me," I responded.

"Maybe you should sit down for a while." Solomon sat me down in a chair, and I could hear him whisper something to Eric. I had a keen sense of hearing when I was under the influence.

"Can you stop giving her drinks now?" Solomon whispered to Eric.

"She's just having fun, bro, relax," Eric responded back.

"Just don't give her anymore to drink!" Solomon demanded.

"All right, fine." Eric sat down next to me, and I could feel his hot beery breath in my face. "Do you wanna dance, or go outside or something?" he asked me.

"No, I don't feel well." I could feel his lips touching the skin of my ears and the side of my face. With what little energy I had I pushed his face away.

"Maybe we should go outside." He grabbed my hand and tried to get me up.

"What are you doing?" I heard Solomon's voice, now speaking to Eric.

"I'm just trying to get her outside," Eric said.

"Leizel, do you want to go outside with Eric," Solomon asked me.

"No, I wanna go home," I said.

"You can't go home. Come on, I think you had enough, and you had a long day. You're tired." He walked me up the stairs and into his bedroom. "Just sleep it off before you leave; I'll come up and check on you in a while."

"How can you check on me? You're busy with Cherri, what if you're busy with her and you forget about me?" I knew he knew what I was implying.

"I'm not going to be busy with her. I'm going to take care of you. Just go to sleep," he said.

I turned over, and soon enough I had fallen asleep. I was asleep for a while, but then I began to hear someone call my name. "Leizel?"

"Solomon?" I said.

"Yeah?"

"Is that you?" I asked.

"Yeah, shhh." He put his hand over my mouth.

With my strength I pulled it away for a brief moment to ask, "What time is it?" I could feel him tugging at my clothes, feeling his cold damp hand on my stomach and moving in different directions. "What are you doing?" His hand went back over my mouth and the other one struggling to open my jeans.

There, in complete darkness, I had the weight of his body, his beer breath and his cold clammy hands controlling his own selfish desires. I felt tears trickling down my face and imagined them dripping off the muzzle of his hand. I squirmed as I could, making it hard for him, but the more I did, the harder he pushed his hand onto my mouth and face. I felt and tasted blood. The weight of his pressure shifted and I froze, and I just let my tears express the poignancy of what God had bestowed upon me. I kept praying to God that he would stop. I kept apologizing to God for having kept my temple clean and now it was tainted once again. Why would He allow this to happen?

Three or four minutes of what felt like an eternity was halted by the light that shined through the opening door, and there was this image of a tall shadow that lunged the weight from my body, and I rolled over to hide the evidence. I slid myself on to the floor hiding on the side of the bed, the lights came on and there I stared at Solomon with Eric in his fists, as blood and tears of humiliation, yet relief, soiled my face.

I cannot quote what Solomon said in anger and frustration, but he dragged Eric out of the room demanding him to leave, and I had buried my face in my hands and cried with more anguish. When I looked at my hands I saw blood; my lip was bleeding from both my biting down hard on it and Eric push-ing it into my teeth. I rolled under the bed. How could I show my face downstairs? I was sure by Solomon's hostile approach to getting Eric to leave, everyone wanted to know why. I would not be the one to confirm anything. I heard Solomon call my name, but I had thought it was him before. I did not dare breathe or make a sound. Perhaps he would think I left already or was in the restroom. He turned out the light and knocked on the rest-room door, calling my name. I rolled out from under the bed, and as Solomon opened the bathroom door to check for me, I ran out of his house and to my car. I could not face him, not then, not ever, although I knew that I could not run and hide forever. He did not chase after me. By the fact that I had evaded him, he knew I just wanted to be left alone.

I crawled in the back of the car, behind the driver's seat on the floor. I lay fetal position in the feet compartment and once again continued to shield my face and wept to God. I had changed myself for God, and just like that He had made me suffer and sin. I cried myself to sleep, and when I awoke and crawled over the seat, there was something placed on my windshield. I assumed it was from Solomon, but I turned on the wipers to dislodge it and as it blew away, I drove away. I drove to Judith's house. I had tried to relay the painful ordeal to her, and she heard me blaming God for allowing this to happen to me.

"It wasn't God, it was the enemy." Judith and I always used the word enemy instead of "devil" or any of his other inter-changeable identities. "The enemy is jealous of how much you love God and how much you have changed for God. He wants to shake your faith. He knows that God has something really special planned for you," Judith explained.

On the one hand I believed what Judith had said, but on the other hand the agony, humiliation, and confusion I had felt provoked a different feeling in my actions. After this event, I withdrew again into isolation. I was just immune to everything and everyone. Everything inside of me was violated, my body, my heart, my mind, and especially my soul.

With a month left of the semester, I ignored Solomon when he was in my presence. I know it was not him, nor his fault, but who was I supposed to blame?

I had gone to a party with my college friends where I met this guy who was a friend of Lily's. He liked me. We spent a lot of time talking, and he offered to take me home so that I would not leave early. He walked me to my door, and we sat on the porch for a while and we started kissing. *He* asked *me* to slow down and that was when I realized that I no longer cared about conserving myself for God. Why should I? He had already taken away what I was saving. What was the message He was sending me? What would I say this time in confession? How would I confess this if it was not my sin? The damage was done and the message that this is all I will ever be worth was sent. I believed it and my decisions began to reflect this belief.

In that month I focused on school and my responsibilities at Saint Ambrose. I was working on the next part of my life's plan, which was applying to graduate school. I was going in three directions, which were journalism, education, and creative writing. Lastly, I continued my communication with Elijah through e-mail. I was looking for a sense of positive validation, and focusing on my career goals was the only success on which I could always count. Elijah's perception of me was always positive as well. He had seen something different in me that I no longer saw in myself. He, without knowing it, was rebuilding my self-esteem. In his emails he would say such things as how he took for granted my goodness when we were together and now he regretted not always being good to me in return. He would predict how one day I was going to be someone special and important because of all the hard work and effort I put into school. In my e-mails there were times when I expressed my sadness and confusion of life, and my loss of faith in humanity. Sometimes I wanted to run away from this place. Once again, his positive energy would lift up my spirit, inquiring what could make me sad, how he had never seen me sad in all the time I was in Oaxaca. Again he would remind me that I was a hard-working person who would go far in life. He wondered what could have possibly happened to crush my spirits to a point of despondent despair, but I never told him.

We told each other our dreams and goals, and his were always to learn English and come to the United States of America. He knew that he would do it. He made me believe that I could do anything I wanted. He said he knew how I felt sometimes, but your strength is in your own thoughts. If you think you can do something, you can. At times he would ask me to send him letters and cards, because it was my words that encouraged him to stay focused and do what he had to do in the present to reach his goals in the future. So I crafted beautiful, carefully worded cards with creative designs and letters for him to admire, as he pictured me taking time out of my schedule to think of him. With every e-mail, the one thing he would tell me was that he admired me. He also encouraged me to stay focused on school, because it would get me far. I used Elijah as a journal, recording all my thoughts.

Once again I was at an anxious point in my life where I wanted this part to be over and be able to start something new. I was one semester away from finishing my bachelor's degree and start graduate school. I was disconnected from God, but I felt not through fault of my own, now even more confused as to how God worked. What did He want from me? I tried to be strong and stand with Him, but something had shaken my faith in Him that was beyond my control, or so I thought. The more time that passed, the more Eric's atrocious attack resonated in my soul, and I could not balance the person God wanted me to be and the person I felt I already was.

In my last semester, I only needed three more classes to graduate. A week or so into the semester, I had showed up at the newspaper office. Outside the media building I saw Solomon's car parked and assumed he was on air with his Spanish rock show. Was the devil with him? I wanted to crawl back into the floor of the backseat of my car in a fetal position as I had done that night, thinking about having to see him again. I went back into the newspaper office and resumed my station, greeting everyone, and many already on edge because of deadlines, scrambling to fill in space.

"I need an interview for our artistically inclined piece," said Amy, the Arts and Entertainment Editor. We often did profile pieces on students so that we could both fill up space, and more people would want to read the paper if they or their friends were in it.

"The guy who is doing the radio show right now is a graphic arts major. Go ask him to do it," I suggested.

"That's so perfect," responded Amy, and then asking, "What's his name? Do you know him? Will you go ask him?"

"Just stick your head out the door and ask the first person to come out if their name is Solomon. I'm pretty sure they're almost off the air," I said.

"What if it isn't him?" Amy said.

"Then the real Solomon will reveal himself." Sarcasm has always been my defensive mechanism to mask my unhappiness, that and isolation. Some people are blessed enough not to have to use their defense mechanisms, and others accept that they will always be like that. I did not want to always have to be like this.

We heard the door open, and Amy jumped up to look out and watched them walk out.

"Two guys are walking out," Amy said.

"Ask them which one is Solomon," I said.

"Which one of you is Solomon?" she asked.

"He is," one of the guys responded.

I could only guess who that was. They both walked into the office. When I looked over at them, Solomon had a new sidekick with him. Thankfully it was a mutual friend of ours from, *Poder*. They both greeted me and I said 'hey,' but I did not make direct eye contact with either one of them. Amy explained to Solomon what she wanted to do, and they took his picture, asked him several questions about his major, and he was done. Before he left, he asked if he could speak to me, and so I reluctantly stepped outside with him.

"What's up?" he started.

"Nothing."

"Why haven't you been around? Some of us have been trying to call you over break and stuff and you're not answering," said Solomon.

"I went to Mexico with my family." I really did, but nothing there was worth mentioning. The one thing I wanted to do was see Elijah, and it had never happened.

"Well, why aren't you talking to me? We can talk about what happened," suggested Solomon.

"Because I don't want to talk to anyone. I don't want to talk about what happened," I said, with hostility.

"I'm sorry about what happened. I just want to help you," he said.

"I don't want your help; I don't want anyone's help. I just want to be left alone!" I said.

"You're acting like I was the one that hurt you," he said.

"No, I'm not. If I were, I wouldn't even be having this conversation with you. Look, don't worry about me; I'm fine, and I don't need anyone's help or sympathy. I just want to be left alone. That's all." I walked back into the office and saw that Amy had uploaded Solomon's picture on all of the workstation computers, including mine. "Why did you do this?" I asked her.

"Because I'm not sure which page I want to put it on. We're not sure about how the layout is going to go," she said.

So every time I did work, there was Solomon's image reminding me of something I wanted so desperately to forget. The one thing I was grateful for was that he did not bring the devil with him. That was considerate of him. Deep down inside I knew that was the kind of man he really was. I was just so devastatingly disillusioned about life and men, and maybe even God. Maybe I should have told him how I felt about him from the beginning. What was the worst that could happen?

I began to have this unusual relationship with God. I found myself often telling people like Elijah and Judith to never give up hope, and give your worries to God and pray to God and He will listen, but then I didn't follow through in my own life. Was it my heart, broken and shattered to one million pieces? Was it my soul, abandoned and wounded from life's confusing disappointments? Was it my mind, telling me that what happened to me was my fault and that I deserved it, that I will never be worth more than the value others have forced upon me? I know it was not all people. It was one person that severed the grip with which I held on to God. What did that say about my relationship with God?

As much as I wanted to ignore Solomon and my feelings for him, he was constantly thrown in my path. He would walk into the computer lab where I was working. Immediately I sensed his aura. His soul quietly called to me. We made eye contact, and I was hypnotized by the swirling sea of his eyes. I could not stand to be in the same room with him. I kept it all within me, and it was overwhelming. I had often admired him, and he had perhaps saved me from something devastating, although too late. I should see him as an even greater savior of my life, but I was not worthy of his love. He deserved better. Someone less complicated. All this time, he had developed a relationship with Cherri. Now it had been several months, and he and this girl had been carrying on in a relationship. Where did that leave me? I had made a mess of my life, and deep down inside I felt that it was God that had complicated it.

It was the weekend of my birthday, and I got an e-mail from Elijah saying that he knows I am doing well because I was an angel, and angels always have to be well; little did he know! That weekend I went to a conference with the group of *Poder* from our college. The conferences are basically workshops that teach leadership skills in education, politics, and media to Latinos. Just other avenues of how we could become successful in the American society so as not to fall into the lost hopes club as so many of our counterparts have. Once the workshops are over, they usually host dances so that people can keep themselves entertained and stay out of trouble, mainly to avoid big after parties. Unfortunately, everyone still had them, and our group was no different. Although Cherri did not go to the conference, because she did not attend school, she showed up to the after party, and so in order to cope with her presence I numbed myself with alcohol. I remembered what had happened the last time I handled a situation like so; this time I was not going to trust anyone, and I was not as vulnerable as I had been once. I had been conserving myself for more than a year, and that was no longer the case.

I had met this guy who was a model, pure visual perfection. He was beautiful from head to toe. I had learned that I had an outer beauty that seemed to be more important to people than my inner beauty, and so I decided to become as shallow. He was rare and original. He had very thick black hair with blue highlights interestingly constructed on his head. He had light green eyes that glowed like lightening bugs against his pale perfect complexion, and naturally red, full lips. He was over six feet in height like a Greek or Roman statue, including the perfection of his well-sculpted body. I was no longer the one that was shy and vulnerable. If I saw something that I liked, I wanted to get it.

"Hi, I'm Leizel," I said with an interested smile.

"Jeremy," he said

"What school are you from?" I inquired.

"I came with Robert and John." He did not want to come out and tell me that he came from a community college.

"So what does someone as perfect as you do with your life? What are you going to school for?" I asked.

"Well, actually right now I'm just taking my gen-eds, but I model. I'll eventually try to become a professional model," he explained.

"I can see that; you're pretty hot!" I had no shame. I just did not care about anything anymore, what people thought of me, of being rejected. Even when I did not take the chance I was being rejected, at least this way I would not be stuck wondering what if!

"Want me to get you a drink?" I had taken the script of the devil. I was in a room of mostly Jeremy's friends from school, and so I had grabbed his hand and took him to where Solomon and our other friends were. "In here, you can have whatever you want, or just hang out with us."

"Oh, cool," he said, innocently.

The typical activities that went on at parties like this were people playing drinking games that included cards and memory, which is why after a while no one would win, because their memory was no longer in tact. I had learned from Eric that most guys had an agenda about what they had in mind after the after-party; they mentally marked that "agenda." I had done the same thing to Jeremy. I was very attentive to what he wanted. I was also watching Solomon and Cherri interact. I hated it. I got a little teary-eyed watching them, acknowledging that our friendship was so far from where it had been. After a couple of hours, people were vomiting, disappearing, and falling asleep, and Jeremy said that he wanted to go to sleep in his room.

"Do you want me to walk you to your room, or are you okay on your own?" I asked him.

"Actually, I have to get my stuff in the car, but I don't even know where I'm parked and if I can find it on my own," he said.

"So you want me to go with you to find your car?" I offered.

"I have to go to my room to get my keys," said Jeremy.

"Do you know where your room is?" I almost felt sorry for him. I felt somewhat guilty, because I could see that even though he was very attractive, he did not seem like a very strong and confident person. I felt like a panther hunting her prey. We managed to get him to his room and get his car keys. We spent about twenty minutes trying to find his jeep. Neither one of us were wearing long sleeves or a coat, and it was about thirty degrees outside.

He found and unlocked the door. "Just come in, so we can warm up," he suggested. We sat in the backseat as he gathered his things together from different parts of his jeep. He hastily threw everything in and now had to pack it all. When he felt that he had everything stuffed in a duffle bag, he asked me if I was ready to go back, and that was when I kissed him. I was physically infatuated with him. Our carnal entanglement was savagely surreal. I was not feeling anything emotionally. My weakness was back, but for how long this time, and could I ever return back to God?

We spent a little time together the next day; he had given me his contact information. I never used it. I felt for the first time I had gotten someone I had wanted and not given into someone that had wanted me. I was always used to being the one put on a pedestal, which I now believed was never there. I had the opportunity to see someone that I wanted and play the conquering game and know the satisfaction of winning and moving on to the next victim. Although Jeremy had been the first win, I played the game at least three or four times after that. I had also felt shame, which was the main reason why I did not call Jeremy or any of them. Why would they want someone that had no self-respect? I felt as though someone else was inside my body and I was battling with them to have control.

By this time my e-mails to Elijah were few and far between, and so were his. A week later I had received my last letter from the last graduate program. I had to make a choice of what I was going to do with the next stage of my life, wanting what God wanted of me. I did not get into all the schools to which I applied, and I had debated about journalism and education. I did have a back-up plan in case I had not gotten into any schools, and perhaps it would have made my life easier, but that was never God's intention for me. He had to continue to challenge me, for He had great plans for me, and I was excited to know what they were. I needed some time to pray about His next plan for me.

And soon enough it was spring break. I would get to spend more time with Judith. It seemed like we had such different lives now. We had gone out to a club, just us, while her husband stayed home with their sons. We had fun, going to the local places, running into old friends and dancing. The last place to which we decided to go, I had run into a very old local friend, Luke. I was happy to see him, especially because of the fact that God and I were not together anymore, at least not when it came to the relationships in my life. I know that He would not approve of Luke, but there he was, standing right in front of me. When we made eye contact, we shared the same ear-to-ear smile, as if we were one, looking into a mirror. We were drawn to each other as we had always been, and we embraced, passionately. I kissed him, the way we used to kiss, and told him that I had missed him so much. I did not care; I did not want to hold back my feelings. Deep down inside I knew Luke was not the one, but he had always inspired me in many ways. We agreed to stay in touch, but for how long this time?

Judith was surprised at witnessing the magnetism of our reunion. "Wow!"

"What?" I said.

"I can't believe how when you guys saw each other, it was like, bam! You just instantly connected," she commented.

"I know, crazy, huh?" I said, excitedly.

"Do you think it's a good idea, him being back in your life?" she asked.

"No! But I don't care," I said.

I missed having someone to think about and admire. I had to be realistic about the fact that Elijah and I would probably not see each other for while, possibly ever. As it was, I could not believe how long we actually continued to keep in touch since I had left. How much longer could I continue to write him not knowing if I would ever see him again? Solomon and I seemed to be in a very different place than we once were. Luke and I were always in the same place, no matter what. I could not say that about anyone else.

I would not listen to God about Luke, but I would listen to Him about my career. I had felt that He was telling me to serve Him by becoming a teacher, and so I made that decision. Journalism was something I enjoyed, but I had changed my mind about choosing it as a career. Teaching would allow me to focus on my professional goals of helping Latino students go to college. It would help me understand why we do not take advantage of opportunities. It would help me change the culture of the lost hopes of Latino communities. It would allow me to serve God first, so that together we can achieve my professional goals. Where I was disappointing God was welcoming Luke back into my life. Did I know that Luke and I would reunite? Eventually. I knew that one day I would want to seek him, but our fate beat me to that. I wanted to be around him and people. He made me feel happy after having suffered such an awful ordeal, as well as losing both Solomon and Elijah. He called me about ten days later, and we spoke about spirituality and the soul. He said that he had been reading the Bible. It was during the week, and so that weekend he had asked me if I would like to see him and, I did.

We had agreed to enjoy each other's companionship. I no longer desired to be in a relationship with anyone. My love, passion, and desire for a person of the opposite sex could never exceed that of which I possessed for my dreams and goals. Especially at this point, I could no longer trust men. I could never have the courage to surrender myself completely. I concentrated on finishing school and prepared for graduation. I was grateful to know the next step awaiting me to move me closer to my ambitions. I was grateful to God for moving me in the right direction. This was what was best for me.

By the summertime, I had seen Luke a few times; I went to a party that he and his friends were having and was only there about an hour. I reacquainted myself with our old friends and watched Luke make a spectacle of himself, and I did not know what to make of him. I wondered when Luke would find God, and perhaps we were both on the same level of our journey to learn to believe in God: we wanted to be with Him, but there were so many temptations against us, and very few people around us not tempting us. I know that I was at a point where I was using Luke as much as he was using me.

A few days after the party, I went to spend some time alone with Luke. "What happened to you at our party?" was the first thing Luke asked me.

"I left!" I said.

"Why did you leave so early? I was looking for you to talk, and James and Deacon said you had already left," he asked.

"Yeah, I was bored. I didn't really know many of your friends very well. I talked to some people, and then I was tired. I was at a graduation party earlier. That's why I was there late and only stayed for a short while. I drove myself, so I didn't want to drink," I told him.

"Wow, that's seems really responsible," he said.

"I guess." I was so uninterested in this conversation with him.

"Well, what else have you been up to? How was your party?" He told me he would not be able to attend because he was going to be in a wedding the same night.

"Everything was good. Thank you. I am very happy about finally graduating. I can finally use this time to ponder greater interests such as my existence," I said, with light sarcasm.

"Really?" Luke asked surprisingly.

"No, not really. I'm happy and excited about graduating," I said.

"I do, sometimes," he said.

"Yeah?" This did not surprise me. "Have you ever seen my son?" he asked me.

"Not really," I said.

"Not in person, right?"

"No," I said.

"Do you want to see my son?" he asked me.

"Is he here?" I asked.

"Yes."

"Is he sleeping?" I asked.

"Yes," he said.

"I don't want to wake him," I said reluctantly.

"You're not going to wake him up. Come on, I want you to see him." He took me to the door of his room. It was low-lit due to a night light. There was his seven-year-old son, whom I had heard about so much; a life of which I had never been allowed to be a part. He was the most important human being in Luke's life, and then he looked at me and said, "There's the answer to my existence. He's got my big ears and big, boney feet." He kissed me on the forehead and said, "Okay, that's enough!" We stopped gazing upon his little creation and resumed our time together. He wanted me to tell him all about my party, and he told me all about the wedding he attended. He said he liked the wedding because he had to dress formally, and he rarely ever got to dress like that. He showed me the suit he had worn to the wedding.

"If I had known that we were showing off outfits, I would have worn my party dress," I said.

I felt as though I had out grown Luke, as though he no longer gave me the feeling that he once did. I had not heard from Elijah in several months. Solomon and I had not talked in over a month. He attended my graduation party, but other than that I felt there was no other reason to see him. I guess the good news was that he was not with Cherri anymore, good news for someone. I missed him more than the others. His friendship had meant so much to me. I did not have a reason to push him away. He was an angel who had saved me and would always remain as such, in my heart and in my soul.

The Angel That Has Captured My Soul

I dreamt of an Angel with deep sea eyes
and glowing brilliant skin.
His lips were inviting,
like the color of forbidden fruit.
The angel called to me,
gently whispering my name,
as though walking on glass.
The angel was he who captured my soul.
In reality he is a sincere and sheepish man.
He listens with an open soul,
and you cannot help but fall inside.
His gentle touch greets my hand,
and sometimes it caresses my shoulder.
He is like an angel, for he protects my soul,
most of the time.
For I have once or twice felt the pain of resentment

shooting from his lips, piercing my unsuspecting soul
that lay wounded like a hunted fawn.
My soul has been taught to forgive,
for it knows love conquers all.
So, once again my heart will find itself
in the possession of the angel
of which I have dreamt,
The angel that has touched my soul.

I waited out time to get to my new phase in life, graduate school. I wanted so much more out of life. Perhaps it was time to see eye-to-eye with God. I wondered if I was spiritually ready to move forward. I tried to understand it all, and prayed for a kind word or inspirational vision to send me back to God, but instead, I ran right into the arms of the devil himself.

LORD, REBUKE
HIS REIGN

> One evening David rose from his siesta and strolled about on the roof of the palace. From the roof he saw a woman bathing who was very beautiful. David had inquiries made about the woman…. Then David…took her. When she came to him, he had relations with her, at a time when she was just purified.
>
> 2 Samuel 11:2-4

The summer before graduate school, like every summer, I went to Mexico with my family. My father asked me to stay an extra month or so with my grandmother so she would not have to be alone. Ironically, I was being asked to watch over my grandmother, or keep her company, when it was she who felt that she had to care for me. I had already begun to feel like an adult since I had returned from Oaxaca, graduated from college, and had been accepted to graduate school. I was beginning to give myself some kind of worth. I was looking forward to my future and being in my sanctuary was a strong beginning for a fresh start. Sometimes I could not believe how far I had come in my life.

I was spending time with Alejandro while I was there. I called him to let him know that I was staying for awhile, and he was excited. He asked me to accompany him to an end-of-the-year dance for law students. We made a date for later that week. He attended a branch of the University of Guadalajara that was located in Ciudad Guzman. It was located a half hour from the *pueblo,* so I had to take a bus to get there. I grabbed the 6B and got off on the second stop once the bus entered the city. He said I had to walk a block down. He was walking toward me dressed in a pair of jeans and a bright orange shirt that was nicely tucked. He showed me around the university, some classrooms, the library, and the computer lab. Then we left campus and he showed me where he lived and introduced me to the host family with whom he stayed. His body language was odd. He seemed excited, but he never touched me or tried to hold my hand or anything. It felt awkward, and I was not sure if he had an interest in me beyond friendship. At one point he grabbed the back of my neck. I pulled away from that and told him I hated that. It was like someone was trying to physically control me. After we left his house, we went for breakfast at a quaint, little restaurant not terribly far from where he lived. This was where we spent a lot of time talking, mostly about politics and topics that we always discussed. I know it was his interests, but frankly I found it a little redundant and boring, and I did not feel any physical chemistry with him. I thought he was cute, but he was so boring. I wanted to give him the benefit of the doubt, and maybe if I showed a little more interest he might feel more comfortable. I called him a couple of days later to tell him thank you and that I had fun. He said that he was studying and now was not a good time.

Hannah was presently working on an associate's degree to teach pre-school and was nearly finished. Her school was in another town, and she was having her graduation dance in a week and wanted me to spend the night out there. She told my grandmother not to worry about me, but I was more worried about her. Since she had been alone, and now that she was getting older, she had fallen down the stairs, fallen into an open pot hole, and managed to have an armoire fall on her. So if anyone had to be worried, it was me.

On Friday I caught the bus to go to Hannah's school. She was going to meet me at a certain spot. It was a few hours away, and it took me a couple of buses to get to her destination. I saw her waiting outside a store for me, and that was when I knew I had safely made it. She helped me with my bag and gave me a hug. Her hair was done fancy, but the rest of her was in waiting to be ready for the big dance. "How was the ride over? I'm glad you made it; I was a little worried," she said.

"It was good. You gave me really good directions," I said.

"I'm glad. The dance is in about two hours. I'm not sure how long you need to get ready. Did you bring the dress?" she asked.

"Yes, I have the dress. Your hair looks cute."

"Thanks, one of the girls did it.

Hannah's dance was a lot of fun. I went because it was a very important night for her. I tried not to attract attention to myself. I was used to getting attention, but I felt as though tonight I wanted to be a wallflower. I was still feeling a sense of withdrawal, and here I was completely surrounded by strangers with the exception of Hannah. Sunday morning, Hannah came back with me on the bus. She finished her degree, and the graduation was in a few days. She would return back with her family. "Leizel, did you have fun last night?" Hannah asked me.

"Yeah, your friends were very nice. So, what are your plans now that you're done?" I inquired.

"I don't know. I have been trying to find a job, but I am having a lot of trouble. My parents and I were able to get a visa, and we might actually go see my brothers in California. They only plan on going for a few months, but I might just stay longer," she informed me.

"Well, why would you want go to over there when you just finished school?" I wondered.

"It's only an associate's degree to teach pre-school. I can't get a job, anyway," she said.

"Where do your brothers live exactly?" I asked.

"Outside of L.A.," she said.

"Which of your brothers are out there?"

"All of them. Noah, Michael, Anthony, and his family," she said.

"Jacob?" I asked.

"Yeah, he's there too. Noah is the one that is always asking about you," she told me.

"Really? Jacob never asks about me?" I asked curiously.

"As far as I know Jacob has never asked about you. He seems like he is doing really well though. Like he grew up a little and is more mature and responsible."

Later that week, I had another date with Alejandro. I do not know if it was a date or not. I was not quite sure what he had expected of me. He came over and asked me if I would mind walking to the *centro*. "No, it's fine, I don't mind walking." When we got to the restaurant, I was disappointed in his behavior.

"Miss, can I get another beer?" Alejandro asked of the waitress.

I whispered to him, "Do you think I could get some more water?"

"The waitress is right there, why can't you tell her?" he responded.

"I asked you to do it for me; is that a big deal?" I asked.

"No, but is it a big deal to ask for it yourself?" he retorted.

"No, you're right," I said.

"Well, I could do it for you, but I thought you were this great feminist or something," he said.

"It's fine, I don't want it anymore. I was finished anyway."

"Well, anyway, I wanted to talk about the dance this week-end. I was hoping maybe you could stay the night with me. I mean, it is going to end pretty late, and there aren't going to be any buses or anything that come back here. It'll be too expensive to get a taxi," he said.

"I don't think I can stay out all night. I would feel bad leaving my grandmother alone. She might not think it's appropriate," I said.

"You're a grown woman," he curtly mentioned.

"She is old-fashioned, and whether I agree with it or not, I have to respect it. I'm staying in her house," I said.

"Well, I was really hoping you would stay the night with me," Alejandro whined.

"I don't even think I'd be comfortable doing that. Why is it a problem that I come home when it's over? I can just ask someone to pick me up; it isn't a problem for me to get someone to do that," I said.

"Well, we'll figure it out." When we got back home, he told me he would call me the next day, and he did, only to deliver some "bad news."

"It's just that when I went to reserve the tickets, it was too late. They were already sold out," Alejandro informed me.

"Really? So not even you're able to go?" I asked.

"Well, I don't know yet. I'm gonna see if any of my friends can help me out," he said.

"Well, I hope it works out for you," I told him.

"I'm really sorry. I'll let you know if anything changes, but I'll call you when I get a chance," and he hung up.

Was it coincidence? All of a sudden the tickets were sold out because I would not stay the night? Why did he want me to stay the night, anyway? Even though we had known each other for a while, I did not know him very well. What did he think I was going to do with him? It just made me sad. I did not understand why these kind of men sought me. I kept feeling that God was challenging my self-worth. It made me continue to believe that no one looked past my physical beauty and all I was worth was my outer appearance. I continued to blame God for my lack of self-worth. Then I would remember what Judith had told me about the enemy. Is it the enemy wanting me to believe that God did not love me? I hated this battle for my soul. I was not always a strong enough soldier to handle it. I guess I did not have the knowledge and strength to fight the enemy.

Solomon sent me an e-mail letting me know he had been trying to get a hold of me for a while until he realized that I was in Mexico. I responded briefly. I had nothing to say to anyone. It was just like him to continue to persist to save our friendship, but I felt so humiliated and defensive. I did not want his pity. Part of me wanted to go to confession before I returned to Chicago and start my relationship with God all over again, but the other part of me was still extremely wounded and wanted to keep hurting myself. Ultimately, I went back to Chicago without absolution, which meant I was still hurting emotionally and spiritually.

I spent my last night before I left for graduate school with Luke. He called me, wondering what I was doing, because he missed me while I was gone. "Do you wanna come over?" Luke asked.

"Not really," I said.

"Why don't you wanna see me?" he asked, offended by my rejection.

"I'm just tired," I said.

"What if I pick you up?" said Luke.

"Fine."

When I got in his truck, he said, "You look good. I'm really excited to see you. Are you excited?"

"Yeah, it's cool to hang out and stuff," I said.

"You're not excited. You didn't say you were excited," he said.

"I'm excited, okay? I missed you," I said.

"That's better," he said, more at ease.

I had challenged myself to get straight A's in graduate school. I had never done it before; I had never even thought of doing it before. While in school, I did not know what to do with my social life. I was swiftly taken by all the knowledge I was learning about "minorities" within our country and what people in *Harvard Journal* and the like thought of Hispanics and African Americans, which was an interesting perspective. It took me a little over two hours to drive into the rural part of the state to go to school. At one point in my undergraduate college career I was very political, and learning about the educational injustices made me have that feeling again. I felt a sense of passion in me to help and serve the "lost hopes" communities, which I knew was part of God's plan for me. But the articles I would read perturbed me. I was ignited with a new sense of fire to move into the direction in which God was guiding me to make a difference. I had a mission that I would be a great student so that in turn I could be a great leader of God. God had begun to rebuild my faith in Him, how I wanted to serve Him. I knew I had my own personal issues, but He knew the strength I possessed to go in a direction toward Him for rebuilding my life, rather than in the destructive direction that many people in my shoes had already chosen. I did not want to allow myself to be a victim or to take the blame, I wanted to be a crusader for change in the name of Christ, but if I was lost, how could I be a leader?

After about three weeks of this intense feeling, I went home for Labor Day weekend. I spent Sunday night with Luke, and after that, it would be a long while before I would see him again, mainly because of school. I ignored outside distractions from men. I would occasionally receive e-mails from Alejandro. I never responded. I did not want to think about him or Luke or Solomon. I even got an e-mail from Elijah about once a month. None of these men mattered to me any longer. Whether I had feelings for any of them or not, I knew that whoever God was talking about in my premonition, it was not the time, and so none of them mattered. Each month went by and I had ignored my personal life. Although I had not felt a sense of absolution, I still tried hard to live life with God on my side, or shall I say with me on His side. At times it was emotionally difficult.

Over Thanksgiving break I had received a phone call from a number I did not recognize.

"Hello?" I answered.

"Leizel?" someone on the other line said.

"Yeah?" I said.

"It's Hannah!" she said.

"Hey, where are you calling me from?" I said, surprised.

"I'm calling from California. Someone wanted to say hi to you," said Hannah.

"Hello, hi, it's Noah, how are you?"

"I'm good. How are you?" I said.

"Good. I was just thinking about you and wanted to talk to you. Just to say hi and see how you're doing," he said.

"What have you been up to?" I asked.

"Just here! Is it okay that I called you? Can I call you again sometime?" Noah asked.

"Sure, why not?" I had put his number in my phone to have the option of deciding if I wanted to answer on future occasions. Hannah had gone to California as she said she would. She was staying with her brothers. On different occasions when I was in Mexico, Noah would call home when I was at their house so that he could say hello to me. It seemed as though every now and again he would remind me that we had shared something special, which for me was my first kiss. But that was the past, and I had to focus on the present.

Grad school was a wonderful experience; it did prevent me from having a social life, but it became my social life. I liked it; it gave me a sense of purpose. I always felt like God and I were on the same page when it came to my career and educational goals. I went out with other graduate students and had friends, but I liked focusing on something that I knew I was doing right in the eyes of God. Graduate school was a life no different than what I had done in the past. I had a full schedule of six classes and an internship and was part of a graduate Latino organization that took on a number of projects that helped the increasing number of the Latino immigrant population in the college town. In which case, I helped start a tutoring program at one of the community schools.

When the first semester ended, I had finished school with four A's and two B's, and so the goal continued. After the first semester ended, I went to Mexico with my parents. I did not see Alejandro. I ignored every male I possibly could. On New Year's Eve, for an hour and a half I sat in my sanctuary, a church, the church where I first felt the presence of God, and all I did was think. I thanked God for the many blessings He had bestowed upon me in the year. I accepted everything and wanted to understand why certain situations in my life had resulted in disappointment. Yet I was grateful for finally having reached one of my most difficult goals, and that was to get a college degree from the community of lost hopes, solely to turn around and have the honor of not only continuing my education at a great university, but for God guiding me to realize our destined professional goal.

Over spring break I was home working on my research project for graduate school. I visited the local high schools in the Hispanic communities. During vacation, I was lying in bed one night, and Noah called me. I answered the phone in order to avoid thinking too much about other topics. "Hello."

"Hello, who is this?" he said.

"Who is this?" I asked.

"I don't know if I have the right number," he said.

"Well, who are you trying to call?" I was not sure if he was just playing games with me, but it did not seem like something he would do.

"Well, where am I calling?" he asked.

"Where do you wanna call?" I asked.

"Can't you tell me who you are?" he said.

"You called me; you should know who I am. Who do you wanna talk to?" I said.

"Leizel," he said.

"Well, I'm Leizel."

"From where?" he asked.

"Well, where do you wanna call? Who are you?" I asked, realizing it was not Noah.

"This is David," he said.

"I don't know a David," I said.

"Just tell me where you are? Where am I calling?" he asked.

"You're calling Chicago," I said.

"Chicago? And this is Leizel?" he repeated.

"That's right. So if you're done wasting my time, 'David,' I'm gonna hang up now," I said.

"Wait, I know who you are," he said, quickly.

"Well, I don't know who you are," I said, getting ready to hang up the phone.

"You're my sister's friend, Hannah's friend. I'm her brother Jacob. My brother Noah must have had you in his phone. He gave it to me because he went to Mexico for a few months. There is this girl, Leizel, from work that me and my cousin are trying to get a hold of. Do you remember little David?" said Jacob.

"Yeah," I said, interested.

"He's right here with me. Do you remember me?" Of course I remembered Jacob, he was the one on whom I had an intense crush, the one I really liked when I was supposed to like Noah.

"Yes, I remember you," I said.

Right here is where I play the memory montage in my head of all the funny and cute little moments we had shared together throughout the years. We talked for a very long time that night. This went against all my defense mechanisms of being vulnerable, but it was mostly I who spoke for nearly four or five hours that night. I did not get that feeling of fear of hanging up thinking that we would never talk again. I had so much inside of me to say, and he was listening. He actually asked me to be his girlfriend and started showing jealousy about why his brother had my phone number in the first place. I told him that he was absurd and that we did not even know each other anymore, because it had been too many years since the last time we saw each other. He told me that he had always had feelings for me, and I told him that I myself also had a little crush on him, because he was so much fun and so funny, but I told him people change. He insisted that he was the same person that I had a crush on many years ago. He was still funny. He only called me one other time after that, sometime in May. It seemed as though I talked a lot more than he did. I felt as though I had someone who liked to listen to me talk and hang on every word I said.

Although the semester had ended, my professor wanted me to continue working on my research work, so I was not going to be able to spend time in Mexico. It was unfortunate, too, because my grandmother had passed away, and my parents were the only ones that flew to Mexico. It was the first time we did not drive as a family. I still had not reached my graduate school goal. The second semester I was one "B" shy of straight "A's".

Hannah called me every now and then and asked me when I would come to California to see her. I contemplated it. I told her that it might be a good idea, after I finished my research work, since I did not get to go to Mexico. By then Jacob had called me again, encouraging me to go visit as well. He wanted to see me, but he frightened me. He seemed so persistent about wanting to be with me. I wanted to go to California to see my friend. I needed a vacation; I needed a change of pace and scenery. So I took a two-week vacation to get to know California and its people.

When I arrived at LAX, both Jacob and little David were waiting for me. Hannah had a job at a dry cleaner and was working. Just looking at both of them, I was more attracted to little David than Jacob. Little David had transformed into a handsome young man. He was still very light in complexion, with light brown hair and squinted eyes when he smiled, but he had grown a little and thinned out in his physique. Jacob was very muscular, thick-bodied like his sister, but had more muscle than fat.

During the day I went out with both of the guys, because Hannah was working. We would go to lunch, go bowling, and play pool. There was an awkward interaction between the three of us, everyone on their best behavior, minding our manners, careful of offending each other. The first Saturday night we all went out to a club, and that was when the dynamics changed. Hannah danced with her boyfriend, Adam, and Jacob rarely ever danced, I was told. So David and I spent most of the evening dancing together. Toward the end of the evening as the dance floor was overcrowded with syncopated bodies, it forced us closer and closer. I felt him pulling me in tighter, and his face touched my cheek. Then he kissed me and we just made out until the end of the night. I wanted him to kiss me because I was attracted to him, and I no longer cared about anything that would happen. I was not as strong to follow God in my personal life, as I was in my professional life. When we got home, Jacob and Hannah went to bed and David and I sat outside on the balcony and talked.

"Are you mad?" David asked me.

"No, I'm not mad. Why would I be mad?" I asked.

"Because of what I did?" he said.

"What did you do?" I asked him.

"I kissed you," he said.

In my mind I responded that I had let him, and how I had kissed him back. "No, I'm not mad; I'm a little hungry." He took me to get something to eat, and then we came back and sat outside and ate our food and talked about random topics until four in the morning.

"Hannah said you wanted to go to the 105 concert. I tried over and over again to call for tickets, but I never got through," he told me.

"Really? That's sweet." I looked up in the sky and noticed something. "Where are the stars? There's no stars in the California sky. I need to gaze upon the stars."

"Is there anything else you want to do while you're here?" he asked me.

"I like beaches." The last thing I said to him was, "Would it bother you if I asked you not to tell anyone about what happened." It was like this encounter went from zero to one hundred in a matter of hours. I did not want to be overwhelmed by it.

"A little, but if it's what you want, then it's okay," he said.

Because of my sleep schedule and his work schedule, the next time I saw him was Monday early evening. He said he had to drive out to Long Beach to pick up a mutual friend of his and Jacob, and would I like to ride with him. His friend did not get off work until nine, which gave us about three hours to kill alone. Because of the last thing I said, there was tension between us. We walked down the beach and then to the bridge to look over the water. We sat down on a bench and talked about our childhoods in Sayula as neighbors. The wind along the beach made it cold. He put his arms around me. "Is it okay if I do this?" David asked.

"Yeah, but why did you ask?" I said.

"Well, you said you did not want anyone to know. I thought maybe it was just a one time thing," he said.

"I just don't like people in my business, judging me. It doesn't have anything to do with you personally," I told him.

"So I can kiss you again?" He asked.

I smiled. I was attracted to him, but I felt emotionless. I liked him, but on a very superficial level. I remembered the conversation we had in Sayula when he told me he was coming here. He worked in a restaurant as a cook now; I felt hypnotized by him. I liked the feeling that I had knowing that he wanted to be with me. So I made out with him again. We went back to the car, and we made out more intensely where I could feel him kissing my neck and his hands wandering. I pushed him back and pointed at the clock, indicating that we had to go pick up his friend.

That evening he and Jacob went out with their friend, and Hannah and I just hung out. She looked at me and gasped. "*Uhh,* Leizel, you should be ashamed of yourself."

"What are you talking about?" I said, unsuspectingly.

She dragged me to the bathroom, and I looked in the mirror and saw that he had given me a very round raspberry-red reminder of our previous encounter. I gasped and responded, "I am ashamed of myself!" I spent that time explaining to Hannah what had happened on Saturday. Apparently no one had noticed.

David worked mostly nights and weekends, and Jacob worked random days and random nights. It made it easy for David and I to spend alone time. He drove me up to the mountains, and we watched the cascading water falls. He and I sat on a rock, me in his embrace, just feeling the summer breeze, and feeling swept away. I felt very emotionally disconnected from my body. There was someone holding my body, loving me, I guess. Someone was touching me, but I felt nothing. A girl pulled up in a rage with her truck. She got out, played some girl power Alanis Morissette song, and wrapped herself in a blanket. David and I watched her and after the song was over she got back into her truck and left. I knew how she felt, but I envied her more for having the strength to come up here alone. When she left, he held me tighter.

I looked out at the peaceful mountains, waterfall, sky, and then I said, "There are stars in this California sky."

"You wanted to go to the beach, so I took you to a beach. You wanted to see stars, I brought you to the mountains to see stars. I knew you were coming, and I wanted to make everything perfect for you," he explained.

I smiled and said, "okay." He had been awaiting my arrival, and that made me curious.

The next day he took me to Universal Studios in Hollywood to see more stars. We spent everyday together, and he opened up to me about all his issues with his family and his work. The relationship just moved very fast, like it was my present life, and my life in Chicago never existed. He said that he felt like we were on our honeymoon. I latched on to his physical body. It was easy to be with him and enjoy his company without being emotionally attached. When the time ended, he took me to the airport and called me later that night to see if I got home safely. I could not believe that I went through this two-week relationship; it seemed surreal. I just felt like God was nowhere to be found anymore. Did I make Him go away? Did He forsake me? I know He is not supposed to, but I did not feel Him inside of me; I felt soulless, Godless, and that was why I was able to fall in love in two weeks, to leech onto someone else and forget all about the plan, God's plan. My body became an abyss, and was now the battlefield for God versus the enemy. I was going to finish school, but I was lost spiritually, especially since I had one year left of school and was not sure what I was supposed to be doing for God anymore. I remember Judith talking to me about a passage in the Bible that referred to not being able to see past the trees, because there is no light. I could not see God's light anymore, beyond the trees.

The next morning when I woke up in Chicago, I wondered what I was supposed to do with myself now. Judith called me to see how my vacation went. "Did you have fun?"

"Of course I had fun," I said.

"Do you feel nostalgic?" she asked.

"I don't think so," I said.

"You sound like you're nostalgic," she informed me.

"Do I? Well, I just got back. I don't know yet, I guess," I responded.

"Well, come by later today when you get a chance so we can talk," she said.

"All right, I'll stop by later."

I started to unpack and put away the clean clothes and start a wash for my laundry. I looked at all the little souvenirs that I had brought back with me. I thought about California and the weather, Hannah, and David. I loved California. I felt like it was an alternative sanctuary to Mexico. I had decided that when I finished graduate school in a year, I would move out to California. I felt happy every morning I woke up in California. In my first year of graduate school and the research I had done, I learned so much about the propositions of California's educational system and how they affected the Latino population.

David called me about three days later. It was good timing. It gave us both a chance to reflect on our experience and figure out what we wanted. "Hello?" I said.

"Leizel, it's David. How have you been?"

"Good, just trying to get back in the swing of things here, you know?" I answered.

"I was just working a lot, trying to get my mind off of certain things," he said.

"What's going on; is everything okay?" I asked.

"Yeah, but I miss you. When I dropped you off at the airport, I never felt that awful leaving someone, or watching someone leave. And I had to leave home, I had to watch my brother leave home. This whole week without you I just felt lost," said David.

"Well, things did seem to move pretty fast because of the short time I was there," I said.

"I just thought it was gonna be a fun visit of hanging out, but it turned out to change my life. I really want to see you again. I can't stop thinking about you. I hope we can be together again. Aside from being pretty and fun, you're intelligent, and serious when you have to be. It's just that I really want to be with you. I love you," he professed.

"I had fun, and I miss you, too," I said. I liked the thought of having a boyfriend and not having to show him that I loved him but just tell him I did and act like I did.

"All I'm asking is that you consider keeping in touch with me and see where it goes," he said.

All I said was, "Okay." Don't get me wrong, I liked David and the nice things he did for me, but I was scared and scarred. I did not think I could ever be passionate about a man again. And could he be mature enough to say he loved me and mean it?

"Just think about maybe the next time you can come out here. I'll even help you pay for the plane ticket," offered David.

"All right, I'll keep that in mind," I said.

"What else can we do?" he asked.

"Let's just take things moment by moment and not get so caught up in the future," I suggested.

"My brother always tells me that I think too far ahead in the future and that I need to focus more on the present," he said.

"Really? That's funny, because my sister used to tell me the same thing. So let's just take their advice," I said.

I was in love with David when he was around or when we spoke, but my emotions responded to the old adage, "Out of sight, out of mind." It had been a year, last Labor Day, since I had seen Luke. I had been home for Labor Day weekend and I ran into James at a club. We went to Deacon's house afterward, and he asked me if I wanted to see Luke.

"When's the last time you talked to Luke?" Deacon asked me.

"I don't even know. It's been a year since the last time I even saw him," I said.

"Do you want to see him? He lives down the street now. I'll walk you down if you want," Deacon offered.

"Who does he live with? What if he doesn't want to see me?" I said.

"He lives with this idiot!" And Deacon slapped his friend in the back of the head. "He'll wanna see you," he continued and grabbed the key to walk me to Luke's house. He went in first, because it was pretty late. Two seconds later he came out with Luke. "I'm going back. You know how to get back, right, Leizel?" Deacon asked.

"Yeah, I think I'll be okay," I said, smiling.

"I'll walk her down later," Luke said.

"Tell James not to leave without me, Deacon," I yelled.

Luke grabbed me by the hand and snuck me into his room. "My son and his cousins all fell asleep in front of the TV. He had a little slumber party."

"That's cute," I said.

"Man, wow! How long has it been?" Luke asked.

"A year," I answered.

"You look so good; I always love seeing you," he said, excitedly.

"I betcha do!" I said.

"Whatever, we don't have to do anything if you don't want. I just missed you, that's all. How is grad school?" he asked.

"It's good, I'm learning a lot and plan to move out to California after I graduate," I told him.

"Are you serious? I've been out there a few times. I like it. Can I visit you?" he asked.

"I don't know. I kind of have a boyfriend out there," I informed him.

"Then why did you come here?" Luke asked me, confused.

"Because I wanted to see you; I missed you. We don't have to do anything, right? We are friends," I reminded him.

"You're right, I do like talking to you." And then I grabbed him and kissed him. We made out for a little bit and then resumed our conversation.

"So when did you move in here?" I asked him.

"About six months ago. It was about time I grew up I guess, huh?" Then he started kissing me.

I did not feel bad about what I was doing. I did not know what I was doing, and I did not care. I was not supposed to be with anyone until after I graduated with my master's degree, so none of this mattered. I knew that Luke was not the one. I had learned to release much of my inhibitions with Luke. He taught me to live a life with a certain sense of freedom, and I was appreciative to him for that. I released all my past emotions within Luke for the last time and knew that it was time to move forward and discover who it was I would ultimately find. The down side of it was that we never got past that imaginary level of comfort the whole time we were in each other's lives.

David and I talked once or twice a week on the phone from September through December. I acted like I was in love with him. It was hard to explain. I was attracted to David, and I loved that he was so in to me. It made me want to be in love with him, or trick myself into being in love with him. Throughout the semester, I lived as though I was in love with David. But in reality, I had no room in my heart for love anymore. He just kept opening up to me in our phone conversations. I felt it was my job to listen.

"Leizel, I have something important to tell you, and I don't want you to find out from Hannah or anyone else."

"What's up? It sounds serious. Is everything alright?" I asked.

"Do you know the reason why I had to come out here? Maybe my mom told you or something," said David.

"No. I don't know. No one has ever said anything to me about you," I told him.

"I know what I did was stupid, but I didn't know what else to do." I remember he seemed kind of jumpy when I asked him why he was first coming out here. "Well, I got this girl pregnant. I didn't know what to do. I wanted to be able to take care of the baby, so I told her I was going to come out here to work and then send money for her and the baby to come, too. I wanted to do the right thing. But eventually I found out that she got pregnant again, from some older guy, and she married him. That was one of the reasons I didn't believe in a long distance relationship, but it's different with you. I have a son, though. I just don't want you to find out by someone else and feel upset like I lied to you. Or if you don't like it and don't want to be with me, I understand," explained David.

"Well, I didn't know. I'm glad you told me and were honest with me. I would have hated finding that out from someone else. And I can't really be mad at you for something that was in your past, before we were together," I said.

"I knew you would understand. I knew everything would be okay. You know every night before I go to bed, I pray to God that you will keep loving me. I know that you are praying at night, too, and that we'll be praying for the same thing, at the same time," he said.

I promised David that I would go back to California over my Christmas break for a few weeks. Unfortunately, our relationship was very different the second time around. The honeymoon was over. The first day he was mad because when he picked me up two hours late from the airport, I was not in the mood to make out with him in the car while his friend drove. He worked the next two days I was there, so we did not spend much time together.

On his day off, he was supposed to take me to a club or something, and he and Jacob came home late. I later found out from Jacob that they went to a club with a couple of waitresses from their work.

On New Year's Eve, Hannah and I hosted a celebration. Of course, about three of her brothers were there, including Jacob, and a few of their cousins, lots of friends they knew from Sayula that were now in California, and people from their work. She and I prepared some appetizers, salsas, salads, and rice and her boyfriend grilled the *carne asada* we prepared in a lime/orange marinade with my secret ingredient. David was at work, and he got home around six in the evening but was going to sleep because he had to go back to work later that night.

"You look nice," David said to me, finally noticing me.

"Thanks," I said. Hannah and I almost always dressed in red on New Year's Eve, because it is a superstition that the color red on New Year's will bring you the great blessing of love. I told her that I did not care about that blessing and that it was just coincidence that I was wearing a red top, because I thought it was cute.

"I'm gonna be at work," David informed me.

"Why didn't you take the day off to be with me?" I asked him.

"I didn't really have a choice," he said.

"I thought you wanted me to come back to spend time with you," I said.

David stared at me blankly and said, "You better not do anything stupid tonight. I don't really want you drinking with any of my cousins. Maybe you should go to bed when I leave."

"I'm not going to bed before the New Year. Just because you chose to work tonight doesn't mean I shouldn't have any fun."

"Will you just come lay down with me for a little bit? It's still early; Hannah and Adam can finish getting everything ready," said David.

"Okay," I said. He put his arms around me, but I could feel his hands begin to slide up and down my body. David and I shared a tender moment. I went through the motions of making love, believing that maybe I was in love with David, but I did not even feel like I loved myself. This was the first time he had given me any attention in the past four days that I had been here, and I fell into his web of manipulation.

It was like something in him had the power to control me. After he fell asleep I left the room to get ready for the party. With David asleep and Hannah busy with Adam, Jacob was the only person I could trust. Jacob sat next to me the whole night, laughing with me, protecting me. I heard David in the bathroom showering to leave for work. On his way out, he looked at me with disappointment beaming out of his light brown eyes.

Two minutes after midnight, I called David to wish him a happy New Year, but he did not answer. Five minutes later he called me back and asked what I wanted.

"I just wanted to wish you a happy New Year," I said.

"Oh, Thanks, you too. I'll be home at like three or four. We can spend some more time together, okay," said David.

When he came home, a little after three, we were all still out on the patio, eating, drinking, and listening to music. He sat next to me. He gave me a beer and would touch me, putting his hands on my lap, or his arm around me. After about twenty minutes he grabbed my hand and said, "I'm tired. We're going to bed."

"Let her stay," Jacob said.

"Why does he want you to stay? What did you do?" David asked, suspiciously.

"What do you mean what did I do? I didn't do anything. We're just laughing and having a good time," I said.

"He must want you to stay for some reason," David said.

"What do you think it is?" I asked.

"I don't know, but I want you to be with me, okay?" he said.

"That's fine," I said.

Initially, David was acting like he did not want to be in a relationship with me, but now he was hording me from everyone else, acting like he owned me.

The next morning on New Year's everyone either slept past noon or got up early to go to work. I got up with David before he went to work. We ate breakfast, and he left, and Jacob was the only one home.

"Wanna go upstairs? Everyone is up at my cousin's hanging out," offered Jacob.

"I don't know if I really feel like it," I said.

"Because of David? Come on, just have fun," encouraged Jacob.

A few hours later David arrived there. I was outside with Jacob and his brother Michael. "Leizel, are you drinking?" David asked.

"I had a couple of drinks. When did you get here?" I asked.

"Why, did you not want me to come? Am I interrupting something?" he asked.

"No, you're not interrupting anything. I'm glad you came. Are you going to stay a while?" I said.

Jacob got up and went toward the door. "Well, I'm gonna get another drink, does anyone else want anything?" Jacob asked, leaving, as Michael followed behind.

"No, thank you," I said.

David was ignoring him, so I thought I would be polite and acknowledge his hospitality.

"Why are you guys out here alone?" David asked me.

"I just wanted to be in the fresh air."

"Well, why did you even come up here without me? I told you I didn't want you to drink with any of my cousins."

"I came with Jacob. He's my friend, too. I trust him," I said.

Jacob came out on the balcony and asked, "What's going on? Is everything okay?"

"I'm fine. I don't know about David," I said.

"Is everything cool? I'm gonna leave. You guys gonna stick around?" Jacob said.

"No, I'll leave with you. Come on, David, let's just go back to the apartment," I suggested.

I was sitting on the couch when Jacob was getting ready to leave for work, and David was in the shower. Hannah was still out with Adam. Jacob told me, "Leizel, I'm going to work. Call me if you need anything. Okay. I'm serious."

"Umm…okay." He seemed like he was worried about something. Jacob left, and David came out of the bathroom and went straight to his bedroom. He came out ten minutes later, sat with me on the couch, and turned on the television in silence.

"David, what's wrong? Why do you seem so upset?" I asked.

"What were you doing up there? What happened between you and my cousin, Michael?" David asked.

"Nothing happened. I was just up there hanging out," I responded.

"Well, he called me at work saying that something happened between the two of you. That's why I told you not to do anything with them. They can't be trusted. They all say bad things about you, except maybe Jacob," David said.

"If I'm telling you that nothing happened, why can't you believe me?"

"But I specifically asked you not to do it, and you didn't care. I can't ever trust you," said David.

"Why do you think that I did something? You've been suspicious of me this whole time I've been back. Did you do something? Do you think I'd do something just to get back at you?" I asked David.

"Well you weren't even excited to see me when I got back. That's why I went out with other friends."

"Friends? Huh? Did it ever occur to you that maybe I wouldn't enjoy waiting two hours at the airport?" I said.

"I didn't do anything. I asked you not to do something, and you didn't have enough respect to listen," said David.

"I see how it is," I said.

I did see what was happening. Maybe David sensed my lack of emotional connection. I wished David had never made our relationship apparent. It seemed as though I had hurt his ego and he had something to prove to me. All of a sudden his behavior had changed. I felt as though David was the devil himself and I had chosen him. I had been pushed toward him. It was like I was attached to David, but I did not want to be, and emotionally I wanted this relationship to be easy, but I had already complicated it. It was like David was also in limbo emotionally when it came to me. He wanted to be with me, but maybe he realized he could not be with someone like me. I was too much work. He could never control me, as he tried to do.

Once back in Chicago, I began my last semester student teaching. I was still drilling the idea of moving to California into my parent's head. I knew it was the next step that God needed from me. David did not call me that often anymore. Jacob would often call me. He was the one that told me that David was dating some waitress from his job. I reflected on all these strong feelings I had for David, because without realizing it, I pushed him to a limit. I felt sad about what I heard about David. I missed him, but I missed the David that wanted to make me happy, but once he got me, his true colors surfaced.

White Grains (Remind Me) of You

White grains of salt
that touch the tip of my tongue
remind me of my acidic–tasting tears that accrue
because ironically, I remind me of you!
For my favorite breath was of the mountain air
that blessed were we given the honor to share.
Somehow the mountains continue to hover over just me,
but the breath of the air no longer seems to taste as sweet.

White grains of sand
turn into dark footprints of mud with each synchronized step,
that from bottom to top we were joined at the hands,
occasionally at the lips
and eventually I envisioned another way we joined,
since the mind is a quick camera that can record and rewind.
for now we are in an unromantic place
due to the fact that we could not contain our urges like
white grains in a jar
that await impatiently on a table,
for our urges to complete one another were impatient!

White grains of an hourglass
that tick, tick, tick
like a time bomb in my head, heart, and feet.

for they are my map, compass, and road,
perhaps waiting to explode,
to find a code or flip a switch,
just to stop this unpleasant, intolerable, dangerous pitch
that finding you will solve.

White grains of faith
turn into red rubies of a rosary,
when I picture you nights (that once belonged to me)
negotiating with God
that etched in my mind you would always be.
Faithfully, God heard and granted,
for with each mystery I beg of God the same.
I remind Him that if not for me,
would you have even prayed His name?
For we spoke of You quite often
as Your name trickled off my tongue that
Once tasted the…

white grains of your kiss
that I am reminded of when in my hand
but with eyes closed
your kiss on my tongue
is just another acidic reminder of
white grains!

My last semester of graduate school went well. I enjoyed my student teaching. I found teaching was an act. I had a natural knack for putting on a show. Every so often David and I had phone conversations. He wanted to make it apparent that he still had feelings for me, but he realized that he could never control me as he wanted, and even though I had feelings for him, I let him know that he would never be able to control me. Jacob and

Hannah and I would talk every once in a while, too. Since I trusted them so much, it would be them that I would count on in my time of need when I was in California. I looked for jobs online and applied for job openings, and when school was over and I received my master's degree, I went back to California for a week to do some job interviews before I would officially make my move in August.

It was due to the previous feelings of dejection I sought out the solace of absolution to try and decipher the difference between God and the enemy. I needed to find my soul again, and I needed to know I was pleasing God. But I felt that the past several months had been lived in a daze. I was hurting myself and other people in the process. I decided not to drink and go to parties anymore in order to try and see the light, which was God beckoning to me, past the trees to guide me toward the next step of my life. I knew it was California, but what would be awaiting me? I was ready for God to reign over the kingdom that was my body and soul.

OUR DREAMS OF LAND AND LOVE

> Then he had a dream: a stairway rested on the ground with its top reaching to the heavens…. And there was the Lord staying beside him and saying: "I am the Lord, am the God of your father…. The land on which you are lying I will give you and your descendents. These shall be as plentiful as the dust of the earth, and through them you shall spread out east and west, north and south. In you and your descendents all the nations of the earth shall find blessing. Know that I am with you; I will protect you wherever you go, and bring you back to this land. I will never leave you until I have done what I have promised you."
>
> Genesis 28:12-15

The start of my summer after finishing graduate school, I went on job interviews in California. This step in my life was meaningful. I wanted to reconnect with God. I had made it this far with Him. I finished college and a master's degree and was excited to see what He had in store for me next. As always, I had the strength and discipline of following the plan for my career, but often the enemy would intervene and confuse me. The enemy would steal my strength and self-esteem, and I made decisions that would favor him instead of God. Sometimes I wished that

I could hold God's hand as He walked with me on a new journey. As I stretch my fingers open, I imagine His power giving me strength and courage, igniting my spirit. I want to feel His embrace when I am afraid and when I am thankful, but I feel it within my soul. Hand in hand, both God and I approach my life together. I remember that there is never anything to fear. I knew I had to make the effort to accomplish what God needed from me and leave my fate in His hands. Despite the fact that I looked forward to venturing out into God's plan, wherever it took me, I wanted to enjoy these final months with my parents. I may not mention them often, but I am who I am because of them, which is why I mention who they are in the beginning. They are my beginning. I would not have accomplished God's plan if not for the spiritual and financial support of my parents.

For a week in June, I came out to California for my first few interviews. I prayed to God for the perfect placement. I had sensed quite often that He had prepared me for this step, that there would be many lives to touch. The two interviews that I had, I did not feel anything. I figured if that was where God wanted me, I would get the job offer, but I was not sensing anything spiritual, at least not with the job search.

The day I arrived in California for the interviews, Jacob picked me up from the airport. It was pretty early, and Hannah was at work. David was sleeping. I was still hurt by the way he and I ended our relationship. I resented him for the way he tried to treat me. When he woke up, we greeted each other cordially and talked about what I would be doing in the next few weeks. When our conversation was over, I knew it was not me that had interacted with David, it was God. If it were up to me I would not have had the strength and goodness to treat David the way God wanted. So I let God intervene in my place. It was my first test of distinguishing God from the enemy. The enemy would have fought with him or blamed him, but I trusted God to handle that situation for me. It was the enemy wanting to disrupt my soul, wanting to entice me into his world. It drained me spiritually to let God intervene in situations where it seemed easier to do what the enemy wanted. Me, without God, I would have shown my aggression, because I still felt the pain or humiliation he caused me. Later that day after I came back from the park, where I went for a jog in order to gain a sense of freedom and empowerment, I was running and Jennifer Lopez's song *Alive* was playing. I felt myself running toward the clouds, or floating toward them, like God was calling me to that and providing me with a sense of power to overcome my spiritual struggles. I felt that it was a premonition, a vision that I would see again indicating I was heading in God's direction.

Unfortunately when I got home, David came home with his present girlfriend and locked himself in his room. No one else was home, so I locked myself in the bathroom and called Judith. Superficially, I thought how much prettier I was than his girlfriend, and in better physical shape, but what had it all gotten me? I felt like sometimes I got hurt because people only admired me for what I was on the outside and no one ever thought about who I was on the inside. Does my physical appearance have a stronger presence than my inner soul? God, what can I do to reverse this? Sometimes I think how I look pretty on the outside, but the inside is spiritual turmoil and no one can see it. Do they even care? Although I felt drained, I knew it was due to God's weight in my soul. There was a war going on inside my soul.

Later that day, Jacob and I went to play pool.

"I told him he was stupid for being with that waitress from his work. She only calls him when she knows you're in town. She's already engaged to some other guy." Jacob was trying to make me feel better.

"I don't even know her. Why does she care who I am and what I do?" I asked.

"I don't know, at first he wouldn't go out with her because of you, but he always falls for her tricks." Jacob dropped his little black Bible. "Oops, I always carry it in my pocket and read it whenever I get a chance. My goal is to finish reading it, the whole thing some day," said Jacob.

"Really? I have a similar goal. A friend from grad school gave me a Bible for graduation, and I have been reading that. Hopefully some day eventually I'll read the whole thing cover-to-cover, too. I'm sure it'll take years," I said.

"You don't have to worry about stuff so much. Just leave it in God's hands and read your Bible and see what God has to say to you every day. That's what I do," he said.

"Jacob, do you ever feel like you know what God wants from you, but it clashes with your own feelings about what you want?" I asked him.

"I know I have done things that hurt God, but He always forgives us and helps us get back on track, no matter what." Although he did not answer my question, he did seem to make complicated concepts sound simple.

We went back to the apartment to catch the World Cup games. He and I were getting tired, falling asleep. I was lying on the love seat and he was lying on the couch. He excused himself to the bathroom, and I ran to the longer couch and stretched out my legs and lower back. When he came back he was asking me to move back.

"Just let me have it for a little bit," I whined.

"Come on, I'm tired. I was working. You're only on vacation," Jacob refused.

"I just feel a little cramped. Just for ten minutes," I asked, but Jacob was being stubborn. He got on top of me and tried to squeeze me out of the couch, and then we made eye contact. Suddenly, Jacob and I began to kiss. I do not know if he kissed me, or if I kissed him, or maybe we kissed each other.

We heard someone trying to unlock the door, and he quickly jumped to his feet and lay on the other couch and resumed watching the game. It was Hannah; she had just returned from her date with Adam. She spoke with us for a bit and then went to bed. As soon as we heard the bedroom door close, Jacob got back up and resumed kissing me. I did not want to take his reaction as an insult, because it was exactly what I had wanted with David, that whatever happened between us, no one needed to know.

The next day Jacob took me to run errands so that I could proceed with my plans of moving to California. As we were driving down the street, a police officer had stopped us. "Can I see your license please?" Jacob gave him his license. "Insurance and registration, please." He gave him the registration but told him that he could not find the insurance card since it was not his car. The officer went to his patrol car.

He whispered to me, "My license is suspended because I got pulled over a few weeks ago by that same cop. That's why I'm driving my brother's car; they impounded mine."

I felt guilty knowing that he was taking me to run errands, and it could get him in a lot of trouble. The officer came back with his license in hand.

"Sir, this license is suspended, please step out of the car." Jacob got out and just then I opened my mouth and let God speak for me again.

"Officer, please don't arrest him. It was my fault. I just moved here from Chicago. I don't know my way around yet. He was going to help me apply for jobs. I'm looking for a teaching job, and he was going to take me to the DMV. He was just helping me. Please don't do that to him; he was just being a good person and trying to help me get settled. Please, I'll feel so responsible," I pleaded.

The officer was silent for a few minutes and then he responded, "I don't know why I'm doing this. I should impound the car, arrest him, and give the owner a ticket for having no proof of insurance. I'm not going to do that. I believe what you're saying to me, and I'm gonna let you go. Do you have a license?" I handed him my license. He saw that it was from Illinois. "You need to drive." He looked over at Jacob. "Sir, you can get back in the car, in the passenger's seat. Next time I won't be so easy. You should thank your friend."

"Thank you, officer. God bless you," I said. In my heart I did know why he was letting us go, because God had intervened.

When Jacob got back in the car he said, "Leizel, I don't know what you did or said, but thank you so much. That was embarrassing."

"Don't thank me, give God the credit. He gave me the words to say, and He influenced the spirit of the officer. There is nothing to be embarrassed about," I responded.

God was in my soul, making and helping me have the strength to do all that I could not have done on my own. I wanted to try more than ever to return to God. There was still a battle of my soul between God and the enemy. I wanted to be with God, but I had to fight the temptation in my life in order to be back with God.

In a month and a half I would return to California permanently. My family helped me throw a graduation/going-away picnic before I left. That was my last weekend home. On Monday, Judith and I drove to California. She agreed to help me drive, and she would fly back once we reached my destination. As I was driving and listening to music, the Jennifer Lopez song *Alive* came on, and there I was, experiencing déjà vu. Seeing myself move slowly toward the clouds, toward God's kingdom, feeling the words move me spiritually toward His plan. I knew in my soul I was in the right direction. God was going to help me fight the demons taking over my soul, and He was going to guide me toward His kingdom. I could not have been more confident in my decision. As Jacob advised, I trusted God completely and did not worry about anything.

I knew it was what God wanted when I arrived in California on a Friday, and by Monday I had a job. It felt right! The enemy tried to throw me off that path. I had called on Wednesday to confirm my Monday interview, and the secretary had told me that the position had already been filled. I called back again on Friday and spoke with the principal, who said he was glad I confirmed that information, because it was not true, and he was still expecting me on Monday morning. So Monday morning I went for my interview, and I could feel the passion of God's words answering all of the questions. Later that afternoon I received a call from the principal, offering me the job, and I knew in my soul this was it. God worked His miracles quickly. But, of course, I never doubt the career decisions He makes for me; it is always my personal life where I struggle spiritually. I knew life was going to be challenging living with Hannah, Jacob, and David, and so I looked for a place of my own as soon as I could afford it.

By the end of August I had my own place, and I started my career as a teacher. It was overwhelming at first, but I felt successful. I tried to be cordial with David whenever I had to be around him. Our schedules conflicted, so I did not have to see him too often. Jacob and I only hung out as friends; very little happened between us while I was still living in their apartment. Once I moved out and had my own privacy, I could focus more on my career and hobbies.

I felt at peace with my new life and knew that I was living for God, and he was blessing me. My next mission was finding a church. I belonged to Saint Augustine's Church all my life, but now I had to find a new house of God. I went to a church that was about five minutes down the street. It was a Spanish Mass. I figured I would stick with what was familiar to me. It was also in the community where I taught, which meant I saw some of the students from my school there. I liked feeling a part of the community through both my job and church; it felt more like home. It reminded me of my mother, who was a teacher and active in our church, both located in Verde Altos. I felt even more at ease now that I had a place to worship.

The first person to come and see me was David. He said that he was on his way home from work and thought he would stop by to see my new place and how I was doing. "Isn't this place a little big for you? Maybe I should move in," said David.

I lived in a two-bedroom, two-story apartment. I wanted an extra bedroom for all my friends and family to have a place to stay if they ever came to visit me. "You gonna pay half the rent?" I asked.

"Looks like I wouldn't be able to afford it," he said.

"Maybe you can just buy the furniture. Sit down if you want. Can I get you anything to drink?" I said.

"Sure."

"So, what's up?" I said, surprised to see him at my place.

"Just wanted to see how you are. You don't come around much. Or maybe I haven't been home when you stop by," responded David.

"Well, since I live out here now, I do have to work. I'm not just hanging out anymore. I go see Hannah sometimes, though," I said.

"Yeah, I know, you don't come and see me, so I have to come and see you," said David.

"I was there for a month, and it was all we could do to get along," I reminded him.

"Well, maybe there's a reason why there is still so much tension between us," he said.

"Why's that?" I asked, interested in his theory.

"Maybe we still have feelings for each other," he suggested.

"Do you still have feelings for me?" I asked him.

"I'm here, aren't I?" was David's response.

"But you're also seeing another woman," I said.

"You're right, but I feel like things should be different between us. I don't want there to be tension. I know I made my own mistakes and you made mistakes. It just seemed like we got together so quick without really knowing each other, like what we felt was only love at first sight," said David.

"I'm sorry I wasn't the person you thought I was and you didn't turn out to be the person I thought you were. I'm fine with it, though, patient, waiting for what God has in store for me. And you, you've already moved on," I said.

"One day you'll find someone that really loves you and you're gonna change," he advised.

"Well, right now nobody wants me," I said.

"Yes, they do, but you…"

I cut him off in mid-sentence. "But they don't want me for how I am, or accept me for who I am."

"Well, when you love them, you'll change for them. It'll just happen." At the time I would have never agreed with him, but if I knew what I know now, I would have thought him quite wise beyond his years.

It was nice to have closure with David. I knew he was not the one, and I had even said that being with David was like being in love with the devil himself. I was curious to see what God had in store for me. To be honest, I was more afraid than anything. I did not even want to know who was out there for me.

On one unexpected night, Jacob called me wondering why he had not heard from me.

"Why are you calling me so late? I asked.

"I just got home from work. What's going on with you?" asked Jacob.

"Nothing, why?" I said.

"Because I don't know what your problem is. Why haven't you called me; are you mad at me? I thought we were friends," he said.

"We are. We're good friends. I'm not mad at you. I'm just busy with work," I told him.

"If you have a problem with me, then come out and tell me," persisted Jacob.

"I don't. I actually miss you. You know you are more than welcome to come and hang out with me here anytime you want," I told him.

Jacob took me up on my offer and began to come over often. His visits were a weekly routine for the next several months. I taught him all kinds of card games. We talked about everything. Often times we would also go out and eat. We went on little outings where I could see the culture of California. We were so comfortable with each other, and more importantly, I felt safe with him. I felt like a child with Jacob. I could let my guard down, and I could leave behind the pain that so many others had caused me. We had a great friendship that took us straight to a very crucial point in my love for God.

Through one of our many conversations, Jacob was asking me what I wanted in life. "I don't know. I guess what everyone wants, to get married and have kids. I finally finished my education and have a career that makes me happy," I said.

"Well, what about me?" he asked.

"What about you?" I said.

"Do you have feelings for me?" he asked.

"Since I was fourteen I've had feelings for you. You've always been easy to talk to, and I can just be myself. You make me laugh. You make me think about God. You're a good friend," I said, evading the question.

"And that's all?" he said.

"I don't know. You allow me to feel complete." I did not want to think about my feelings for Jacob. I did not want to think about my feelings for anyone ever again.

We maintained a friendship like this for months. Over my spring break I made many changes to my soul. Since I had found a church, I had accepted absolution. My mother was talking to me about the concept of a spiritual wheel. By the way she described it, I had come up with my own visual representation of what I imagined its purpose to serve. In the center of the wheel, the core, was God. The outside of the wheel consisted of all the significant things in my life where I needed God's prayers and blessings, such as my family, my career, my students, my finances, daily encounters, and all my future endeavors. In between were the spokes. The spokes represented different forms of how God connected to my inner core and outer world, such as prayer, patience, Mass, the Bible, forgiveness, allowing myself to be used as an instrument, connecting with God's nature, absolution, and many other ways. By living these examples, I can keep the wheel turning. If a spoke breaks, then the wheel will no longer spin, and danger can arise, and my life will no longer run smoothly. It is hard, though, to keep the spokes maintained and the wheel of my spirit rotating. That Saturday night when Jacob was at my house, I shared my spiritual wheel with him, because I was very proud of it.

"Well these are the things that I try to do to stay in tune with God. Forgiveness, praying the rosary, confession, Mass, you know stuff like that," I explained.

"Reading the Bible, like me?" he added.

I smiled, "Yeah, reading the Bible, like you." He was so cute!

"God talks to you through the Bible. He gives you visions," Jacob reminded me.

"Like what?" I asked.

"What He wants from you and the dreams that you want," he responded.

"What kinds of visions do you see?" I asked him.

"Land, crops, lots of greenery. I think about buying land in Mexico, and that maybe He is telling me to do it, that it's part of His plan. What do you think God is telling you?" he asked me.

"I don't know," I said.

"Well, you said you wanted to get married and have kids. Is that the vision that God gave you?" he asked.

"I don't know; it's what I want," I said.

"I want that too. God gives me that vision too, but it has to be with someone that wants the same things I do," he said.

"Like what?" I asked.

"What we like to do, how we raise our kids," said Jacob

"How is that?"

"Well, you know the woman should stay home with the kids. I don't want them to be watched by strangers," replied Jacob.

"I don't want my kids to be watched by strangers either, but it doesn't mean that I have to be the one home watching them," I said.

"Who would watch your kids while you worked?" he asked.

"Why not my husband? Or family and trusted friends. I know I would never leave my kids with anyone I didn't know well, or even if I didn't know the people they keep company with that well. I guess, it if comes down to it, maybe I wouldn't work, to be the one to be able to stay with my kids, to protect them from people that don't care for them. I just would never want my kids to feel abandoned, or for someone to hurt them," I said, agreeing with Jacob, but not for the same reasons.

"Why do you think that cynical?" he asked.

"Because that's what my mother did to me. She sent me with strangers that made me sad; that hurt me," I told him.

"But your mom didn't do anything to you," he said.

"But she allowed it to happen. You don't understand what I suffered because of her decision," I said, not liking where this conversation was headed.

He began to hear the hostility in my voice and said, "But you can't blame your mom for that. She doesn't even know."

"But if a child is crying to a parent about not wanting to be somewhere, or go somewhere, they should listen and try to understand. You know what? This isn't even any of your business," I said anxiously.

"Maybe it isn't, but you know you're sitting here bragging about your wheel and all the things you do, and you still have all this anger inside of you. You don't do all those things you say you do; you haven't forgiven your mother. It's hypocritical! I know that I have made my mother suffer, but she has forgiven me, and she loves me. I know you're confused; I once felt like you. You can't get close to God if you don't forgive," Jacob said defensively.

"It's different; it's just a different circumstance, and you don't understand." I felt all this pain, and perhaps humiliation, and I started to cry. I ran upstairs and locked myself in the bathroom.

He was knocking on the door. "Open the door! Why did you run off?"

"Just go away, leave me alone. I don't want to talk about anything with you anymore," I said.

"That's fine. Just open the door and come out. Stop crying. Calm down and come out," pleaded Jacob.

I heard him trod down the stairs, and the door opened and closed. I waited about ten minutes, and then I came out. I went to the door to lock it, and there he was sitting on a kitchen chair. "I thought you left," I said.

"I just needed some air. Are you okay?" he asked.

I walked to the table, picked up the paper that had the drawing of my spiritual wheel on it, crumpled it up, and responded, "I'm fine; nothing's wrong." I shot it into the waste basket.

He jumped up and said, "What are you doing? You worked hard on that; it's important to you."

"No, it isn't. None of this is important to me anymore," I said.

He fished it out of the trash, smoothed it out, and said, "Please don't throw it away. Go take it back upstairs."

I went upstairs, and when I came back down he was shuffling the cards and dealing them.

That night I dreamt that Jacob and I were gardening in front of a beige house. I saw miles of land, crops and flowers. We had walked in to the house together. I was caring a basket of lilacs, and he was laughing and telling me a joke. All of a sudden we knelt down in front of a picture of Jesus, he slipped a ring upon my finger, and we kissed. He touched my face, and I told him that I loved him and that I promised to serve him. Then I awoke. I knew then that he was the one that God had sent to me and wanted me to serve. But of course the enemy is always challenging those of us who want to serve God, and so the reality of the premonition would not be that easy. Even though I awoke with a resolved feeling, I wondered like before if it was God telling me that Jacob was my soul mate or if it was my inner conscience. I had to have faith and trust God.

I did know, however, that Jacob was working as an instrument of God. It was God speaking to me about my wall of defensiveness. I had realized that often times I blamed my mother for the bad occurrences in my life. I had to forgive her, because I knew she loved me. I had to accept and understand my past. I also realized that perhaps Jacob was the one that God wanted me to serve, because he was helping me get closer to Him. He had the courage to tell me what I needed to hear because he cared about me. I was so mistrusting and afraid of love and getting hurt. Unfortunately, the enemy continued to make the battle for my soul a challenge for God.

A few days later I went to the apartment to see Hannah, and as I was getting there, I saw Jacob holding hands and getting into a car with a girl. Before I left my car, I called the apartment. Hannah answered, and I asked her if Jacob was there.

"No, he just left with some girl. I thought you were coming over," said Hannah.

"I am. I just wondered if he was home because I owed him some money. But it's fine. I should be there in a little bit." I hung up the phone, and I felt an overwhelming sense of spiritual confusion. I watched them leave and could see the happiness in his face, knowing I was the last thought on his mind.

I had to make a decision. I did have feelings for Jacob, and I felt so close to him spiritually. Now however, I felt spiritually disrupted, but he was not doing anything wrong, at least not to me. Maybe he was with someone all this time, or maybe he met someone new that he liked more than a friend. I needed to give him his space. Set him free! Let him go! I wondered if God gave Jacob the same message. When would God let him know?

A few days after that, I was at Jacob's apartment. I left Hannah's room to let myself out as she was getting ready for bed. And as I passed by Jacob's bedroom, the door was slightly opened. I mustered the courage to speak to him. I did not know what I would say, but I knew God would give me the right words. I pushed open the door to his room. It was dark; the only light came from the television.

"Is it okay if I come in?" I asked him.

"Yeah, what's up?" Jacob asked.

"Nothing. How are you? Haven't seen you in a couple of weeks," I said.

"I've been busy, working a lot," responded Jacob.

"Yeah, me too. It's too bad that we're too busy for each other," I said, awkwardly.

"I don't know about that," he said.

"Well, it might feel like that sometimes, but you know your friendship is very important to me, right?" I told him.

"Your friendship is important to me, too," he said.

"I'll always be your friend, and I would do anything for you if you ever needed me, regardless of what my life is, regardless of what your life is. I'll always be grateful to you for all the help you've given me since I moved here, all the time you have spent with me. You have helped me in ways that you wouldn't imagine," I informed him.

"Like how?" he asked curiously.

"Well, financially…and…you helped me understand some of life's mysteries. You extended your hand to me and pulled me closer to God. You will always occupy a space in my heart. I would never turn you away in your time of need." As I was pouring my heart out to him, I could feel myself getting choked up on tears. I could feel the strength of my words drain my soul.

"I'd never turn you away in your time of need, either," he said.

"If a lot of time goes by and for some reason we don't communicate, don't think it's that I'm mad at you. I have to go; I just wanted to say good-bye," I said hastily, wanting to cry.

"You're just going home, right?" I know Jacob did not understand, but I was going to set him free, and if the premonition God sent me was true, he would eventually return to me.

Ode to My Soul mate

Prelude: It's been a week since the news about you and that girl.
It's been a week since I've been confused about you and that girl.
It's been a week since my soul has escaped its shell.
Has it gone to hell?

I believe it's floating aimlessly about the world.
Have you seen it?

We had recently interchanged pieces of our souls.
Do you remember?
Let the story be told:

As my spiritual wheel turned,
you grabbed a hold,
gripped tight
beyond my sight
slipped passed my wall of defensiveness;
slipped inside my spiritual wall of forgiveness.

Through your lips
God's words scolded,
bold,
how I was told,
"hypocrite,
quit
lying: sin,
for there is still anger and pain from within."

With God's palm you pulled me over, past the wall of sorrow and
pain.
Your spiritual faith taught me to regain
inner love, joy, and peacefulness.
With God's strength you broke through the wall of defensiveness.
Pushed on,
pulled over,
stood with me proud and high
in heaven, at His throne in the sky.

Hand in hand our souls connected, looking eye-to-eye-to-eye.
I swam the sky;
soared the sun;

YZABELLE JIMÉNEZ MARTÍNEZ 229

clung to the clouds,
then slept
and dreamt!
A vision of you crept,
your body in my soul
into the plan of God!

Destined are we
as I was blessed to see,
and wondered if this vision was also sent to thee.
Could I be wrong? Wrong to believe?
Wrong not to believe?

He breaks no promises---
as your promised lands
that will succeed,
equal is the soul he has deemed you need.

A slap from the unholy has caused our hands
to loosen their grip.
you let me slip;
a spiritually painful trip.

For you reached in and grabbed onto my soul
and ripped it clean through its mold.
I showed no struggle to hold
on.
Pain had weakened our spiritual bond.

Before I let my soul escape
a spiritual interchange was made with God's strength.
His visions unraveled,
the proof of a journey we were destined to travel.

"I will always be your angel,
ready and willing to give.
I will always be so grateful
that you had taught me to live
in peace with God and within my soul.
I will always be for you
despite the wrong turns that we take.
I will always be for you
despite the mistakes we choose to make.
Delivered in true words to thee.
Is it God? Or is it me?
For you have been promised ownership of the land
that is my heart
and not solely one part."

These overwhelming words of servitude
rung the drips of holy tears
a symbol of hidden fears.
Now courageously proclaimed
I patiently wait to be reclaimed,
for God has already established in His plan of fate
that I have been selected as your one and only
true soul mate.

God then showed me who it was that I must serve, and this journey in itself would be another long road to travel in His presence. What would the journey be like? How will God show me the way? How long will it take this time? I hope you were able to reflect on your relationship with God as you walked with me through mine. I hope I was able to move you at least one step closer to God, to open your heart and accept His unconditional love for you. Although I know I had moved closer to Him, I also knew that I was not where I wanted to be.

Through the journey of finding my plan of God, of completing my promise to Him that I would always serve Him and follow through on what He wanted from me, I had the help of many people, including you. There were people that I mentioned briefly, or that I did not mention at all, but I know everyone is in my path for a reason. Although many names and places had been changed for the purpose of anonymity, there was one name which I had not changed. God's role in my life was not exaggerated, and the situations in which He played a part were not fictitious. He had planned this story for me all along, and our journey together will continue. For I need your prayers and strength now more than ever, as I continue to follow God's plan. Will you walk with me in God's strength into the next oath of God?

listen|imagine|view|experience

AUDIO BOOK DOWNLOAD INCLUDED WITH THIS BOOK!

In your hands you hold a complete digital entertainment package. In addition to the paper version, you receive a free download of the audio version of this book. Simply use the code listed below when visiting our website. Once downloaded to your computer, you can listen to the book through your computer's speakers, burn it to an audio CD or save the file to your portable music device (such as Apple's popular iPod) and listen on the go!

How to get your free audio book digital download:

1. Visit www.tatepublishing.com and click on the e|LIVE logo on the home page.
2. Enter the following coupon code:
   12ad-8da3-4a7e-8c69-35a2-12a6-5d85-b3ea
3. Download the audio book from your e|LIVE digital locker and begin enjoying your new digital entertainment package today!